BARGAIN FOR A BRIDE

MONTANA PASSION: BOOK ONE

AMELIA ROSE

DEDICATION

To YOU, The reader.
Thank you for your support.
Thank you for your emails.
Thank you for your reviews.
Thank you for reading and joining me on this road.

CONTENTS

Chapter One 1

Chapter Two.. 7

Chapter Three 11

Chapter Four 18

Chapter Five 24

Chapter Six 29

Chapter Seven 35

Chapter Eight 42

Chapter Nine.. 47

Chapter Ten... 55

Chapter Eleven.. 60

Chapter Twelve 67

Chapter Thirteen.. 75

Chapter Fourteen.. 82

Chapter Fifteen 90

Chapter Sixteen... 96

Chapter Seventeen.. 101

Chapter Eighteen... 109

Chapter Nineteen 117

Chapter Twenty 125

Chapter Twenty-One 132

Chapter Twenty-Two... 139

Other Books by Amelia Rose 145

Connect with Amelia Rose..................................... 146

About Amelia Rose 147

CHAPTER ONE

The lord of the house seized the sheaf of yellowed papers in his fist, the rough ends of his fingers nearly tearing through the thin sheets before crumpling them in the middle. His rage—a common feature among the men of the Brennan household, as it was often the source of many raised voices among the family and nightmares among the staff— was clear on his face, his ice blue eyes practically burning as his nostrils flared in an effort to slow his breathing. That effort was wasted, and it wasn't long before a pewter mug flew from the table, clattering to the floor by the oversized fireplace, spilling its contents across the stone floor.

Of all the servants lining the hall, not one moved to retrieve it or to clean up the mess. There would be time enough when the master's anger had subsided or after he'd drunk himself calm again, though without his mug, there'd be little chance of that happening. The butler looked at the other servants warily, then filled another mug with ale from the sideboard and slipped it in front of Lord Brennan before jumping back to his position behind the master's chair.

"Who does he think he is?" Ronan bellowed. "My father is in the ground two weeks, and already the wolves come calling, demanding a piece of his estate? I'll not have it! Send word to Lord Macomby that the Brennan lands are not for sale, and neither is the Brennan family!"

Moira turned and looked sharply at her older brother. His strange order could only mean one thing: another marriage proposal. Her rod-straight back wilted only slightly. Her brother was a good man, and his recent bout with drinking was only the result of the strain of stepping forward to fill their father's place at what should have been one of the most festive times of the year. With St. Nicholas Day already past and Christmastide looming, the usual bustle of the holiday festivities were absent this year. There were no decorations for the great hall and no gatherings planned, either for the townspeople the Brennan's watched over or the nobility who would have come calling if death hadn't visited instead.

Now dressed in mourning, the entire household missed both their loving former master and the spirit of winter. There were no sprigs of greenery to liven up the rooms, no spice sachets hung from the doorposts to encourage good cheer. The rooms were as empty as their hearts now that the beloved master had passed.

"Yes, sister, it appears as though Old Man Macomby fancies himself a new wife, a much younger one this time. It obviously doesn't worry him that he is a hunchback and a cripple, so long as he has a pretty young woman on his arm in the day and warming him in his chambers at night," Ronan spat in his fury, snatching up his new mug and nearly draining it in one long gulp. Moira pressed her hand to her mouth in revulsion at both the thought of someone asking for her hand while the entire countryside knew them to be in mourning, and at the thought of wedding and bedding the octogenarian.

It wasn't like Ronan to be so vulgar, and prior to taking to drink the way he had, he would never have spoken to her that way. He'd have shot any man who dared voice such crude words, but she was able to overlook his brutish behavior and count it as the drink taking hold of him.

"Would you leave us?" she asked softly, looking up at the servants. One by one, they turned and gratefully fled the room, hopefully not to take their talk of the family and its woes to the great kitchen below. Moira hated the thought of them whispering behind their hands at the family's misfortune, but hated the thought of them witnessing her brother's recent struggles even more.

The butler saw the servants out then waited post by the door for further orders from his mistress. He wasn't certain that she should be left unattended with a man in that angry, uncontrolled state, brother or not, but knew no household functioned without orders being obeyed. He waited until he met her eye, then waited for her to nod before leaving the room and closing the great doors behind him.

"Ronan, brother... what is the matter?" she asked gently, rising from her seat and coming to stand by his chair—their father's chair, the seat Ronan had tried to avoid until he was cautioned by his uncle that orders for the household came from that place of honor, an honor that belonged now to Ronan whether it pleased him or not.

"It is as I've said," he answered, trying not to slur his words. His bleary eyes didn't even attempt to focus on his younger sister's face, the face that had hovered over his bedside every time he'd been injured or ill. The face that was the embodiment of loving kindness and humility, that was the face he saw every time he even had a passing fancy of running into the city and drinking until there was nothing left of him. He shook his head. "Lord Macomby claims that you and he were betrothed before Father died, that Father was thinking of you even in his last months of illness. As though I wouldn't see to a strong and beneficial match for you myself!"

"But that is ridiculous! Surely the old man means one of his sons, not that I find them much more appealing than their father, mind you, but all three of his sons are older than I! He cannot mean for me to marry him in their stead!" The thought of being the new Duchess of Macomby while her stepsons were easily ten years older than she would have made her laugh if it weren't so despicable to think about.

"That is as his letter states," Ronan replied, holding out the offensive correspondence. Moira shook her head, unwilling to touch it long enough to look at it with her own eyes.

"Father would never have done such a thing, I'm sure of it, certainly not without consulting you in the matter, at least," she replied adamantly, acquiescing to her brother's anger. "And I fail to believe that our father would have even done so without speaking to me. It isn't the custom, I know, but that was his way. We were the light of his life, and he would never have secured a match such as that man for me, and I know he would never have done so without speaking to me."

Moira was near tears, not for her own sinking heart at the thought that her father had entered into an agreement with a veritable ogre, but that he would have done so without her knowledge. Her happiness and Ronan's had always been important to Father, and an unthinkable blow such as this one couldn't be what he had intended.

"I know this isn't Father's wish," Ronan said, seething as he reached for his empty cup. He snapped his fingers for a servant to come refresh it, but finding the room empty, he fell back against his chair instead. "This smells strongly of our uncle's doing. He's been after the estate ever since Father even took to his bed, and no amount of rebuttal has kept him from insisting he is the rightful heir. Father's will cuts him out almost entirely, largely because of his ambitious nature. If there was even a chance that Uncle and his kin would be content with an annual sum, I would gladly pay it. But he will not rest until we're turned out and he inherits it all."

"Oh, Ronan, that's why I've urged you to marry! You must hurry and find a wife, one who will give you an heir of your own. We've money enough, she doesn't even have to bring a wealthy dowry, just find her! Uncle will not let this rest until he has no grounds to say the family title isn't secure." Moira furrowed her brow as she thought about her brother's answer. "But I don't understand... what would Uncle care if I'm married? And to that old monster?"

"Who knows what that monster is thinking? Other than Macomby's other suggestion... if you're not to be his wife, he's calling me out for a duel. And at his age and with the blame being on his failing eyesight, he has foregone the pistols himself and appointed his son—the younger one who has been serving in the British army these *six years*—in his stead. You are to pack your things and depart for Marcham to be wed, or I am to face off for your hand, dragging my coffin behind me."

"Surely you cannot believe that Uncle wants to see you duel for your life," Moira exclaimed. "He is our family!"

"And he is cut off from the inheritance, do you not remember? Everything passed to me; the estate here in Brennan, the home in London that Father kept for his visits to Parliament, even our family's interests in India and in the

Americas. Uncle and his sons will receive a modest annual salary off of the interests of the estate because I felt it only fitting, but having me cast aside would make them the immediate heirs to the entire Brennan fortune. Better men than Uncle have killed for far less, I'm afraid." Ronan sank back into his chair and stared numbly at the fire, the effects of the ale wearing off in a most unpleasant way.

"I'm as good as dead already."

"Don't speak such a thing, brother!" she cried, racing to his chair and throwing herself down before him, clutching his hand in hers. "I'll marry Macomby before I let that happen to you! It is not my wish, not by far, but if it keeps you from your grave…"

"I would dig that grave myself before I'd agree to promise you to that lecherous old man. Do you know how many wives he's had, not to mention how many bastards he's fathered besides?" Moira blushed deeply at the subject her brother broached, but she didn't scold him for it. "If there was an ounce of goodness and generosity in him, he wouldn't keep finding himself widowed. His wives have died in their childbeds for want of even a country horse surgeon, let alone a doctor, as he won't spend a pound to spare them. The talk in town is that they slave away in the sculleries of their households alongside their servants while he rides the countryside, all because he claims they are kept in line by an honest day's work. They serve him as lord and master until their countenances give out because of his harsh treatment. I won't have that for you."

Tears stung Moira's eyes. There had to be a way to prevent both the ill-matched marriage and the duel, but if she knew of any answer, it was kept from her mind's eye, prevented by the rush of emotions she felt at the horrendous news.

CHAPTER TWO

Moira had hoped the following morning would bring sunshine and a better outlook, but within only minutes of waking, she knew that something was horribly wrong. Her ladies' maid, Gretchen, threw open her chamber door and raced to her bedside, dropping into a brief courtesy and whispering urgently, "My lady, please! Hurry, you must wake and prepare. There's a man here to see Lord Brennan, and they're discussing you! There's no time, we must dress you!"

She threw back the covers almost rudely, but Moira knew the girl would never have been so callous if she weren't frightened out of her wits. Gretchen's hands shook as she helped Moira to wash her face, do up her curly brown locks, and change into a gown suited for receiving guests in the day time. They raced through the process before hurrying down the hall as fast as they could on silent feet, stopping in doorways to see that they were not discovered. Gretchen pinched Moira's cheeks to bring color to them in case anyone noticed them, as the lady of the house did not ever look pale.

"You are a villain and a scoundrel!" a man's voice bellowed from within her brother's office. Even through the heavy oak door, Moira could hear the shouting as clearly as if she were in the room with them. Other muted voices murmured their agreement, their words obscured due to the lower volume.

"I'll thank you to leave my house this instant!" Ronan shouted, equally outraged. "No man enters my home and brings this kind of news, then has the daring audacity to speak to me thus! If you have business claims to attend to, you may contact my solicitors in their offices. But my sister is not for sale!"

Moira and Gretchen looked at each other wide-eyed, their fears confirmed. She was the cause of the shouting within.

When the sounds inside the office turned to more shouts and even the scuffling of some heavy furniture against the stone floor, Moira could take it no longer. She threw open the double doors and stood dwarfed in the grand doorway, straightening as best she could to her full height. She held her head high, looking every bit the noble lady she'd been raised to be.

"I understand there is a disagreement in my house," she began in a firm but steady voice, her mother's lessons in composure and carrying one's self coming to mind.

The effect was immediate, and intentional. The men in the room, five or six of them at first glance, all rose and turned toward her, bowing low in the lady's presence, her brother included now that they had visitors. As they looked down, awaiting her word that she would receive them, she took the tiny opportunity to breathe deeply and clear her head for whatever unpleasant business lay ahead of them.

"My, such a loud conversation from so few gentlemen. I had expected to find your office filled to the windows, dear brother, what with all the shouting."

"I apologize, Lady Brennan," Ronan answered as the men stood upright again, using her formal title for the benefit of his most unwelcome guests. "I do hope we did not disturb you from your sleep at this early hour."

"I must confess that I was sleeping when a commotion roused me. I was certain it was wild animals, and came to inform you that we must send out the guard to do away with them at once. Imagine how foolish I felt when I discovered it was merely our guests."

The assembled men alternated between looking duly shamed for having upset a lady, and irritated at having been called animals by the one they were there to discuss.

"My lady," one of the men began, a gentleman Moira had seen among her father's associates. "We have come to discuss the pending marriage."

"Really? You are marrying again, Sir Walbridge? Then you have my heartiest congratulations, although it is usually far quieter a conversation when a man chooses a bride," Moira answered innocently.

"No, my lady, not my marriage, my wife is still quite well, thank you," he stammered, covering his embarrassment at having to be the one to explain. He looked to Ronan for help, but the man just turned away. After all, his sister was putting the men in their place quite nicely without his help.

"Then I'm afraid I do not know to whom I should offer my congratulations," she continued, looking around the small group. They each, in turn, averted their gaze as she looked at them, shamed by their discussion in front of her.

"Who is getting married, my lord?"

"You are, my lady," he finally answered, and if she hadn't known better, she would have sworn that he sounded almost sad at having to be the one to tell her. "You're to marry Lord Macomby by the end of the week."

"And if I fail to comply?" Moira asked, her mask of confident unconcern still firmly in place. She stole a glance at her brother, who continued to watch out the window at some distant scene, his mind elsewhere as he fought to maintain his composure in front of his lady sister.

"I'm afraid, Lady Brennan, there is no choice in the matter. These gentlemen have come to escort you and your brother to the duke's summer keep first thing in the morning. You are to pack your necessary items today."

Her mind reeled with thoughts of escape, but she continued to play the role that had been carefully crafted in her since she was but a babe. She stood erect and unflinching, silently forcing the men one by one to look at her as she waited.

"And how many servants are to accompany to my new home? I will need to prepare their trunks as well as my own."

Ronan turned sharply at what sounded like her resignation to be married, but she turned and left the room to prepare. The men barely had time to stand and bow again before she reached the doorway, her skirts billowing out behind her in her haste to get away.

CHAPTER THREE

Moira dipped the fountain pen into the inkwell at her writing desk and continued the letter, wiping at the tears that dropped onto the fine linen paper as she wrote. She kept seeing Ronan's horrified expression, one that ran the gamut from heartbreak to shock to rage, as he eventually read her words:

> *Dearest Brother,*
>
> *I cannot have it on my conscience that you fought a duel on my account, especially not on the half-truths and outright lies of those we know to not have our best interests at heart. Greed is a powerful force, one that neither you nor I can overcome on our own.*
>
> *I am gone to the Americas this day, and I pray that you not come after me. I beg your forgiveness for the hurt and the shame this will cause you and our family, but I must leave to secure your safety*

and prevent this poorly made marriage. I do ask that you slander my name and report to all that I ran off because you were forcing me to marry Macomby. It is the only way to save us both.

Ever your loving and faithful sister, Moira

She carefully sprinkled the paper with fine sand from her silver shaker, then laid it aside to gather up her things. Moira crept out of her suite and made her way silently to the office where her brother conducted the family affairs, kissing her letter silently before placing it on his desk, once their father's desk.

She peered into the hallway to make sure no one was about, then headed to the servants' galley and waited at the appointed spot. Only moments after her leather shoes tapped against the stone floor, a young woman stepped out of the shadows and laced Moira's hand through her elbow. Gretchen curtsied, then reached for Moira's traveling bag before picking up her own worn case.

"Won't you be missed?" Moira asked her longtime companion in a hushed whisper.

"No, m'lady, I have no one. My parents a' been gone many a year now, and you know me aunt took to her bed last spring and never came up again. 'Sides, 'tis only fittin' that I go wid ya. You can naw travel alone, not a lady of your station. 'Tis not right."

Moira nodded and jerked her head in the direction of the hallway. They stepped into the darkness and felt their way along the stone walls until they finally emerged in an antechamber that would take them to the stables. They swathed themselves tightly in layer upon layer of wraps and cloaks against the harsh temperatures, then set out for the stable.

There, a groomsman had tied the horses to the carriage and was prepared to take the young ladies to the port, carrying them to a new future that didn't involve forced marriages and estates but that still was rife with danger.

By the first light, Moira and Gretchen were safely stowed in the chambers adjacent to the captain's, arguably the safest rooms aboard ship. They were bound for America, eager to put land behind them as quickly as possible. Moira couldn't let herself step out of the cabin for fear of seeing a member of the household race toward the ship on a breathless horse, knowing they would pull her from the ship by force if necessary. Ronan himself would be the first suspect on her list, as she knew he would never let her sacrifice herself for him.

But where will he be once he loses the duel to Macomby's sneering brat? The opponent has fought in the Americas, in the Caribbean, and in India, all trained and outfitted by the British crown. What had Ronan done, except been a dutiful son, a loving and careful brother, and a man with a smart head for business? If he hadn't been so adept at overseeing his father's affairs, Uncle wouldn't even be interested in the estate. It was only because of Ronan's diligence that anyone wanted a stake in his profits.

And he'll be just as dead as if he hadn't earned them a farthing, she thought, the fresh tears welling up in her eyes again. Instead of feeling the sense of adventure everyone else on the ship was feeling—even Gretchen, although the girl was loyal enough to deny it, she was sure—Moira was almost inconsolable at having to leave her home behind.

She read the post bill again for reassurance, looking at the withered document that promised untold riches and land of her own, land that she as a woman could still claim. It clearly stated that everyone was welcome to apply for homestead. Maybe if she could secure property of her own, Ronan could join her and put all of this in-fighting behind them. She would have preferred to see Uncle take all of it if it would save her brother, and they could start afresh in this place called Montana, a place whose beauty surely must match its enticing name.

An agonizing several hours passed before the great ship actually moved away from the port, finally allowing Moira to release the tense breath she'd been holding since first making her decision and packing her trunks to leave her home forever. Gretchen paced back and forth the length of the overly large cabin as the ship crept out of port at a snail's pace, retracing her steps over the length of the good-sized room intended for passengers of Moira's station.

"My lady, you have naw told me what it is we're to do once we reach land," the ladies' maid began nervously. Moira regretted for the hundredth time dragging her longtime companion into this, but it wasn't right for a young lady, especially one of means and allegedly betrothed to an older man, to travel alone, let alone to undertake a journey like this.

"We're to meet up with a certain Mr. Walsh at the land office in New York," Moira explained patiently, knowing that much of that didn't register in the younger girl's mind. Land ownership and ocean travel were concepts that didn't have much impact in a servant's daily life, so it was only natural that Gretchen would have questions and doubts.

"And how did ya hear of this Mr. Walsh? What if he's up to no good?"

"Not to worry, Gretchen, he comes highly recommended by a number of people who were in business with my father. I haven't corresponded with him personally, but I understand he handles the American side of business for a lot of people in my family's circles. Now, let's see if we can walk about the deck and get some fresh air, shall we?"

Their stroll along the railing of the ship would be their last view of the sky for the rest of the four-week voyage. The new steam engine technology had greatly reduced the length of time to make the trip from Liverpool to New York, but even steam engines still had to stop in various ports for passengers and cargo, and they most assuredly couldn't do anything to make the weather any better. Moira and Gretchen spent most of the trip huddled together in their cabin, wringing their hands and fighting the feeling of seasickness brought on by the rough waters, torrential rains, and bitterly cold winds that howled through every rivet in the vessel.

Christmas on the ship was a wretched affair. The ladies ventured out of their cabin only for the meal with the captain at his insistence, promising them it would be alluring enough to raise even the darkest spirits. Gretchen helped Moira dress in one of the few fine gowns she'd packed, having reserved the rest of the space in her trunks for necessary items and simpler clothes.

The captain was right on one account, and that was the extravagance of the meal. But instead of lifting her somber mood, it only made Moira more morose. It was a stark reminder of what should have been taking place right that very moment at Brennan Castle: her father, had he lived, should have been stoking the fire in the great hall and ordering another round of sherry for the glasses. Her brother should have been standing behind her plush chair and asking her if she was warm enough before they both insisted she play the piano and sing carols for them.

Instead, she was seated on a rocking ship with complete strangers who were trying to create a festive air, but failing.

She excused herself immediately after the meal, too weary in her soul and too heartbroken to join in the singing that was planned for after dinner.

By the time the ship reached New York, the two ladies were too exhausted to feel the gratitude the handful of other passengers aboard the freighter felt. Joyous cries from outside their small window let them know when the new country came into view, as a cheer went up from the paid passengers and the crew alike. The storms and high waves had made it a difficult crossing, and everyone was thankful just to have survived.

"Oh, Gretchen, look!" Moira called out, pointing to the city skyline in front of them as they descended the gangplank, following immediately behind a porter carrying the lady's trunks and Gretchen's simple homespun bag. The maid's sight followed her mistress' outstretched arm and took in the sweeping city, far larger than any town she'd ever laid eyes on. Everywhere she looked, rooftop spires on tall buildings brushed the clouds, only to be outdone by the construction of a new, even taller building beside it.

"My goodness, m'lady, whatever would they need with such a great lot of houses? Do you really think there's people in all of 'em?" Gretchen couldn't help but stare at her surroundings, pressing a small hand to her nose as a whiff of rancid air off the bay assaulted her senses. Coupled with the usual noises of a busy seaport, the overall effect was almost enough to make her turn around and climb her way back up to the ship. Only the memory of the weeks of storm-tossed agony kept her from heading back home that very minute.

"Well, it's certainly not like London or Liverpool, but I suppose it suits these people just fine. Come on, let us find Mr. Walsh and get back to the wide open spaces. I need to see some greenery after looking at naught but the cabin walls." Moira paid the porter, who loaded her things onto the back of a waiting hansom cab. She provided the driver with the address, ignoring his look of surprise as they ducked into the covered carriage and out of the cold winter air.

"Are you sure, ma'am?" he asked in an accent that was both strange and thrilling to Moira. "You just don't look the type to be seen in those parts."

"I'm quite sure, thank you. Drive on!"

CHAPTER FOUR

"I'm quite sure that is the correct address," she promised him after he asked for a third time, settling back against the plush velvet cushions of the cab and letting her head fall back for only a second before remembering to carry herself with importance. After all, she was not only the Lady Brennan, newly arrived in America, she was also about to become a landowner, something she couldn't do legally back in Ireland. She gave Gretchen a reassuring look and began pointing out different landmarks she'd read about in the newspapers.

They arrived at the austere offices of the land management department and paid their fare. The driver agreed to wait in front to guard their belongings; Moira may have been born and raised on an immense and therefore somewhat isolated country estate, but she was no stranger to the ways of cities, having traveled much with her father before his passing. They entered the office and announced themselves to the young clerk working behind the brass grated window. He came out and directed them to a rather plain-looking office that held only a simple desk and two wooden straight-backed chairs for visitors who wished to conduct business.

"I'll go let Mr. Walsh know he has company," the clerk said, smiling with something close to devilishness in his expression. Moira and Gretchen took their seats in the two wooden chairs, their small purses clutched between their hands and placed on their laps. Gretchen shook noticeably as her nerves got the best of her; Moira, although excited and somewhat nervous herself, had a lifetime of talking to people beneath her in status, and therefore didn't feel the worry that Gretchen was struggling to hold in.

"Miss Brennan," a loud voice said around the stub of a cigar he gripped between his teeth. "Oh, wait, I'm so sorry, I mean… Lady Brennan. Where are my manners?" Mr. Walsh came around the desk and dropped into the leather chair. "What brings a fine lady such as yourself to our humble land office?"

Moira couldn't speak for a moment, shocked as she was by the somewhat boorish Mr. Walsh. She'd never encountered a man who smoked in front of her, and a cigar at that, as the only men she'd known to smoke opted for pipes and took the activity to another room with the other men, to enjoy brandy and talk of business.

"I've come to inquire about a parcel of land… in the West," she began, recovering quickly.

"Land?" Mr. Walsh returned, blinking rapidly and using his hand to fan his own plume of acrid smoke away from his face. "You want land?" He reached for a stack of papers and rifled through them until a piece of fine linen stationery stuck out from the pile. "Oh, I remember now! I got a letter that said you were coming."

"A letter, Mr. Walsh?" she asked, suddenly afraid. "There should not have been a letter…"

"Yeah, here it is, from a Mister Ronan Brennan…" Gretchen and Moira exchanged a horrified look, but Mr. Walsh didn't seem to notice as he continued to explain. "Says here you've left home with your family's blessing, and that I should be expecting you. He's asked me to help you in any way I can. So tell me what it is I can do for you." He crossed his hands on top of the letter and looked between the two young ladies, waiting for an explanation.

"Oh, I see," Moira said, her thoughts several thousand miles away with her brother, now all alone in the world. She pushed aside the image of him drinking each night away in front of the fireplace, and took a deep breath. "Well then, I've come to inquire about some land, as I stated. I should like to place a homestead claim on a good-sized piece that can be farmed, preferably with enough acreage to lease out the property to tenants."

"Tenants, Miss Brennan?"

"Yes, tenants. I myself have no knowledge, skill, or desire to farm, but I have years of experience in managing my family's property and maintaining a relationship between the household and the farmers in the village. I should like to establish a farm here in America that will let me continue."

"You see, that's the problem, ma'am. That's not how it works here. People aren't heading West just for the fun of working someone else's land. They're staking their own claims and living beholden to no one. We got immigrants every day, stepping off the boat like you just did, pardon my manners, and heading out West to make their own fortune. I hate to tell you this, but you're not going to find anyone interested in signing on to work your land and pay you a portion of it."

"I see, Mr. Walsh. That is an interesting viewpoint. But our farmers in Brennan aren't beholden to us, they rely on us for many things. They're all too happy to return the favor."

"Well, this isn't Brennan, and it sure isn't Ireland, either. You go throwing your fancy title around and thinking people are going to line up to rent space on your farm, and it's not gonna be pretty." Moira blanched at his tone of voice and the threat in his words, while Gretchen slipped a hand protectively through her mistress' arm. "I'm happy to help you with your homesteading, Miss Brennan, especially because I have this letter from your brother saying you're clear to make your choice. And with that ship going down a couple of weeks ago with its banking cargo on board, the whole city is struggling for gold. If you've got the funds to pay the fees and the credit to secure the rest of it, the land is yours. But you have to know you'll be in for a surprise when you finally get there."

She thought about his offer quietly, but finally nodded. This wasn't how she envisioned the process, but it was a small setback, one she could overcome. He left the room to gather the necessary paperwork, and Moira had to put a hand up to stop Gretchen from crying.

The clerk from the window was the one to bring the stack of papers for Moira to sign. She began reading the official documents, but eventually the strange version of English and the legal talk had her already exhausted and disappointed mind swimming. She reached the final few pages, signed them, and stretched her weary fingers before handing the stack to the still-grinning clerk.

"Thank you very much, Miss Brennan... I mean, *Lady* Brennan, of course," he said in a voice that sounded very much like he was mocking her. He took the papers and placed them inside his ledger book, then produced another bound packet of papers for her to look over, plus a small bound volume on what she would need to purchase and know in order to homestead her claim. "You'll want to read these over before departing for the claim. As Mr. Walsh said, the last thing you want is any surprises."

The clerk chuckled at his own joke and left the office, leaving Moira to stare after him in confusion. She turned to the papers and glanced at them, but decided to wait to read through them until she was less tired.

"Now to find lodging, and plan our trip West. We'll travel by train, now that the line extends all the way to California."

"Pardon my asking, m'lady, but how is it that you know all this? Homesteading and train travel and this Mr. Walsh… how ever did ya manage it all?"

"Well, I'll let you in on a little secret," Moira began, pulling Gretchen closer and linking elbows as they walked out of the office and out onto the sidewalk. "I had a good mind to speak to my father and my brother about expanding to America someday. I've been planning on it for years. I knew that whomever I married would be a hanger-on to his own family's fortune. Our land and holdings aren't so vast that I would make a good match. I wouldn't be an asset to some of the larger families, so I have always known that my husband would likely be a second son, even a third, and therefore not stand to inherit his own estate. And with Ronan and his wife—God willing, he should marry soon— inheriting Brennan, I've always thought it prudent to marry and have my husband be appointed to see to the family's interests abroad, either here or in India. We would have our own holdings and our own household, but still be contributing to the Brennan estates."

"That is quite brilliant, my lady! You should have been

born a man, if it's not too bold of me to say." Gretchen ducked her head at having been so outspoken, but Moira only laughed.

"Oh, think nothing of it, Gretchen. You're right, after all, 'tis not fair that a woman with a good head on her shoulders is barred from succeeding due to her 'delicate' nature and the way ladies are viewed. But that's all behind us now! We're in the land of opportunity and there is a bounty of options open to us. The West awaits us, as does our future!"

CHAPTER FIVE

Moira was not quite so optimistic once she saw the accommodations. Their temporary lodging, while far less than Moira could easily afford, would have to do until the train departed the following Tuesday. She was already carefully budgeting for the items they would need upon their arrival in Montana; extravagant luxuries like lodging in the Aster House, which would have eaten away at her remaining funds, especially because Gretchen would have required a separate room in the servants' quarters, were too frivolous at a time like this. She put on a brave face for her maid's sake, trying to remain cheerful as she reminded her that their lodgings would be even more sparse once they arrived at their appointed plot of land.

"Come, Gretchen! We've travel supplies we must gather. We'll wait until we arrive in Montana—how I never tire of saying the name! Montana!—to buy the bulk of our dry goods and equipment, but we'll certainly need more suitable travel clothes for the train journey. I apologize, dear, but it appears that Mr. Walsh didn't book us a private car as the expense was very great. I attempted to pay the difference at the train station this morning, but the private cars are all booked. But it will be more than suitable, I know it will. Besides, we need to plan our funds carefully. We will be fine financially, of course, but I can't know what needs we will have once we arrive, and certainly not once we face the winter out West."

"Will the winter be fierce, my lady?"

"I've heard talk of the seasons and it seems that the temperature is much like home." Moira's voice cracked on that last word, but she cleared her throat lightly before continuing. "After all, we'll be living in a cabin, practically a shack smaller than our carriage house, so I should think the winters would be quite cozy, nothing like trying to warm the stone rooms of Brennan Castle. My only fear is the wind from the mountains, wrapping us in snow that we cannot fight our way out of."

"Do you think we'll have much snow?" Gretchen asked, her eyes brightening. Moira remembered looking out through the windows and watching some of the servants romp and play in the light dusting that landed one Christmas Eve, wishing more than anything that she could have gone out and joined them in their fun. Instead, with her mother already passed away, Moira had to be the lady of the house. She'd smiled watching them, but wished she could have been a child herself instead of a lady.

They discussed what they knew about Montana and America in general, which both admitted was not a lot. They speculated on the things they would see, the area in which they would live, and their plans after staking their claim. Moira was excited about the opportunity to take charge of her own life, and even made the scandalous pronouncement that she might purchase work pants for herself, causing Gretchen to cry out in alarm.

By the time the day had arrived for them to depart, cabin fever had set in again, far worse this time than it had been on the ship. Knowing there was an entire bustling city just outside their doors, and an even greater frontier awaiting them to arrive, made their stay indoors almost unbearable. Between their brief, icy cold walks about the city and their meals taken at the boarding house's dreary, rather dirty kitchen, Moira and Gretchen hadn't ventured too far from the apartments. Their only interactions in the city were limited, as their focus was on their journey.

They finally boarded the train and tried to hide their disappointment at seeing the crowded train car. Barely better than a freight car, their fellow passengers were crammed into the aisles and rows, with those who didn't purchase a seat having to stand. They wedged themselves past the crowds of travelers until they found their seats, collapsing gratefully and overjoyed to see that theirs were situated side by side next to a wide window.

"Here, Gretchen, you take the seat beside the window. We can open it slightly if you feel faint, as the fresh air will do you good once we begin moving," Moira said, directing her maid to the narrow cushioned seat before sitting down beside her. She took their bags and stowed them beneath their feet, then settled back into the seat, eyeing the passengers around her to see who looked trustworthy. To her dismay, much of the group seemed shifty instead.

The train, unexpectedly fast at twenty-five miles per hour, was nearly dizzying with its speed, and more than once, Gretchen had to turn away from the window to avert her eyes from the colors that blurred past. Moira traded seats from time to time, content to let her ladies' maid rest her head on her shoulder while she slept, a gesture of familiarity that had gotten her chastised more than once by some older relatives. More passengers exited at each of the tiny train depots they stopped at, and although a few more passengers came and went throughout the journey, the car was practically empty by the time they'd reached the Ohio Valley.

This went on for days. The ladies made use of the washrooms as best they could, but by the third day, they mourned even the comforts of the slummish boarding house. They took their meals in the small towns where the train would pause for longer stretches, and at the start of the second week of travel, Moira surprised both of them when she let a room for the day, just to give them a chance to wash in a bathtub and sleep in a real bed, even if it was only for a luxurious nap. They barely made the train before it departed West again, but they managed.

"My lady, how is it possible that we haven't gone 'round the whole world and ended up back in Brennan by now?" Gretchen said mournfully, her shoulders slumping from the weeks of riding in her seat. Everywhere they'd stopped and every train change they'd made, she'd stretched and walked, but the miles were showing in her thin frame.

"I understand your worry, but it's for naught. I never would have thought it possible that the country could be so enormous. It makes me worry that Ronan would never find us, if he ever chose to, that is."

"Oh! You don't think we'll never see him again, do you? Surely someone as stalwart as Lord Brennan could move the very mountains that stood in his way to come to his sister!"

"I dare not think of it. My heart is torn in pieces at what I've done to him. Is he sad that I've left him? Is he angry that I've gone against his wishes? I only hope he knows I did it to save his life and the Brennan lands. If I'd stayed, either Ronan or our estate would no longer exist."

It was Gretchen's turn to pull her mistress into a comforting embrace, resting the lady's head on her thin shoulder and patting her arm comfortingly. They'd noticed that every stop brought a rougher and rougher crowd of passengers, none of them women, and they'd tried their best to avoid attention and keep from looking too prosperous. Fortunately, none of the other passengers paid them any mind, all too intent on their own affairs and their own reasons for travel.

The weeks stretched on and the endless miles of country proved just how immense this new land really was. Cities gave way to farms, which gave way to sporadic settlements dotting the landscape, but all the while, Montana never appeared. Rain beat at the windows at times, and every evening, the car was wrapped in eerie darkness as the sun descended. The scant light from the oil lamps on the walls only cast an ominous flickering over the assembled passengers, making the view inside the car even scarier than the view outside.

It was a welcome shock when the conductor shook both ladies gently by the shoulder early one morning before the sun had risen above the horizon. He peered down into their faces with his weathered smile and said those most blessed words: "We're here. Welcome to Montana!"

CHAPTER SIX

New Hope, Montana, had a population of merely eighty-six people, or so the wooden plank hanging by one corner above the unofficial postmaster's house claimed. Moira scanned the train depot for any hint of civilization, and was dismayed to see no one in sight. She pulled the collar of her coat closer to her chin and reached out a gloved hand to point out their baggage to Gretchen.

"Come, Gretchen, we'll find someone to greet us and tell us where we're to go next." She left her maid to oversee the transporting of their trunks, but when she realized there was no porter coming out to help, she bade the girl to give one handle to her. Together, they wrestled all their worldly possessions around to the front of the station, letting them fall to the wooden boards with a loud thud when they took in the town in front of them.

It was barren. Except for a few squat, clapboard buildings, there was nothing to break up the gray countryside, nothing to stop the eye from seeing all the way to the mountains in the distance. A wide dirt path ran between the two buildings, cutting a road far wider than any Moira had ever seen. The reason immediately became clear as she made out jumbles of hoof prints in the frozen road, scars left by what had to have been thousands of cattle.

"My lady?" Gretchen began, but she stopped. She had no question, at least not one she could expect Moira to know the answer to. Moira just stood, staring, taking it all in as she tried to formulate her next move.

"Surely there's a boarding house here," she thought aloud, speaking more to herself than to her maid's unspoken question. "'Why have a train depot, or a rail stop at all, if there's nowhere to stay?"

"We can ask after this man, no?" Gretchen said in a hushed voice, not wanting to draw attention to the fact that they were newcomers and were already lost. Just as Moira opened her mouth to call out to the tall man, the only other soul standing in front of the station, he turned and strode toward them, a look of derision clear on his face.

He stopped only a few feet from them and looked from one girl to the other, his eyes roving back and forth several times before stopping on Moira's. He nodded curtly, no sign of recognition in his gray eyes. A faint scar above his upper lip twitched lightly when he spoke.

"You. You're the Brandon girl? I'll take you. Someone will come along for the other one soon, I suppose." Moira blinked in surprise, trying to decipher his words. His accent was not so unrecognizable as to be foreign; in fact, it felt almost familiar, but the words he spoke made so little sense that surely he wasn't speaking their language.

"I'm sorry? Pardon my ignorance, but I'm not sure what you're talking about," Moira said, standing taller and assuming the same stance she used with servants and business acquaintances of her father's.

"I'm Pryor MacAteer. I'm here to fetch you," he said, as though that explained everything. He paused, then seemed to remember himself before taking off his hat and grabbing Moira's hand, shaking it forcefully by way of greeting. Gretchen reached out her hands to steady her mistress, holding her firmly by her upper arms to keep her from toppling over at the near-thrashing.

"*Fetch* me?" Moira asked. "I'm sorry, I don't understand."

"Oh. Okay. I'm here to pick you up? To take you to my cabin?"

"Why ever on earth would I go to your cabin?"

"Because I have an order here to pick you up? I placed the ad, and they sent you out. I paid your fare, remember?" Moira and Gretchen exchanged quizzical looks, then turned back to the man in the cowboy hat and denim pants, waiting for him to explain. "You are Mara Brandon, right?"

"No, the name is Moira Brennan. Lady Moira Brennan, of the house of Brennan," she said slowly, watching for some kind of understanding to cross his face. It never did. Instead, he reached behind him into a deep pocket sown to the outside of his thick wool coat and retrieved a piece of worn yellow paper.

"I got this here letter in the post, had to go all the way down to the fort to pick it up. Says here that you're gonna be my bride." He held out the piece of paper, but Moira jumped back from it as though he held out a live snake clasped in his gloveless hand. She finally peered at it and sure enough, her name was in faint typed letters across the top of the page.

"There is a misunderstanding, I assure you. I am no one's bride. I left home for this great land specifically to avoid becoming someone's bride! I am here with a homestead claim." She reached into her handbag and produced her own paperwork, thrusting it in Pryor's direction the same way he'd offered up his letter.

He didn't look at it. Instead, he narrowed his gaze as he looked straight at her innocent but determined blue eyes, the wheels in his head turning with this new situation. "I know what's going on here. Don't think for a second that I'm a big enough fool to fall for it, though."

"I don't know what you're saying…"

"You think you can get free passage out here and then turn your pretty little nose up at the contract. Well, we don't take kindly to people going back on their word around here. You signed a contract, and you're gonna be held to it. Now grab your things, we're headed home." He turned to leave, as though he actually expected Moira to follow. Instead, she glanced at her maid and shot her a look that showed her clear contempt for this man, then sat down on her trunks to prove her point. Gretchen joined her in her indignation at being ordered around by this pig of a man, sitting down alongside her.

Pryor didn't bother turning around. He called over his shoulder, "You don't want to be sitting there when the sun goes down. And I can't much promise that you want to be sitting there when the sun is up, either," then kept walking.

"We will wait for the authorities, if it pleases you," Moira called back from where she sat.

"It does not please me," he answered. "Seeing as how we don't have any authorities. You'll be waiting 'til I'm long past need of a wife. So let's go."

"I am staying here. Once you have left, I will go in search of lodgings for my maid and myself."

"There aren't any lodgings, either. You've never been to this part of the frontier, have you?"

"Obviously not. I should think that would be plain to see. Why would I call for the authorities and announce my intention to find a boarding house or an inn if I knew such things would not be available? I think you're taking advantage of my ignorance of the region to strong arm me into acquiescing. And I won't stand for it."

"Lady, you sure talk a lot, but I didn't understand half of what you just said. Now grab your bag and put it in that wagon. We have about a two hour drive to cover before evening chores, and we don't want to do the milking after dark."

"We, Mr. MacAteer? Why would I do the milking with you?" Moira asked, more puzzled than put out.

Pryor finally stopped walking, pausing where he stood for a moment to gather his thoughts. This wasn't working out the way he'd envisioned it when he'd first heard about the opportunity to find a companion. He'd only known two other homesteaders to write off to the city back east for a wife, but they'd both explained how simple the process was, but more important, how happy their wives were to come to the frontier. This wench acted like she'd accidentally gotten off the train at the wrong station. Despite his shy, gruff manner, Pryor had mulled it over for months before ever sending off his letter, and had been just as hesitant about replying when he learned that a woman was headed to Montana looking for a husband. The last thing he wanted to do after waiting for so long was to start things off on the wrong foot.

He walked back to the covered porch of the train depot and stood in front of Moira, looking down at the two ladies where they were seated close together on an expensive-looking trunk. He took a deep breath before he spoke.

"I don't know what kind of confounding thing is going

on, but I have a signed contract for you to be my wife. You signed the papers with your own mark. The papers just arrived this week, with instructions to pick you up on the train. I've been coming to this train station every morning since the papers arrived, on account of I... because it didn't say what day you'd be coming." Moira's angry glare softened just a little. "I've neglected my farm long enough. There's work to be done, and the whole reason for writing off for a wife was to find someone to help me, and someone to be a companion. So far, I don't have a lot of faith that you'd be either of those things."

"Thank you for the explanation, Mr. MacAteer; I appreciate the time spent telling me your side of the story. But I'm telling you that I came out here to claim my own piece of land, not to be someone's bought and paid for bride! There has certainly been some misunderstanding and I assure you we will work to make it right, but until then, I am not anyone's wife, and I certainly won't be doing any milking!"

CHAPTER SEVEN

After such a forceful and confident proclamation, it was with no small amount of consternation that Moira found herself helping with the milking in Pryor's small barn only two hours later. Gretchen wouldn't hear of her mistress actually putting her delicate hands anywhere near the large animal, but she did concede to letting Moira hold the lantern while she set about the task herself.

"'Tis shameful," Gretchen kept muttering to herself. "You, the Lady Brennan, standing in a barn, up to your ankles in droppings! I have never in my life been glad that me dear mother is dead and buried, but I must say, I am grateful that she is naw alive to witness this!"

"It will be all right, Gretchen, you'll see. And we must remember, my title does not hold sway out here. Here, there is work to be done, and it seems that every able hand must do its part."

"But yours is not an able hand, it is a high born hand! Me mother was a ladies' maid before me, and she would have me whipped just for letting you keep watch in here with me! You, having to witness something so disgusting as the milking! I would naw even know how to do it me-self if 'twas not for having to take meals from the kitchen to the farm hands!"

"Tis a shame not of my doing, but being high born seems to no longer be a factor to my credit. In fact, here, it possibly renders me a liability, a mouth to feed who does not contribute."

The term "mouth to feed" was still smarting for both of them, as it was the very words Pryor had used to describe Gretchen. Moreover, it was the reason he gave for insisting that Gretchen would not be coming with them to his property. Seeing no current solution to their problems, Moira had agreed to go with Pryor and make herself useful in exchange for room and board, assuming that all manner of decorum between them would be observed. But Gretchen was a whole other issue as far as their new host was concerned.

"I didn't sign on for two people," he had said while loading Moira's trunk in his wagon, blushing when he realized his words could be taken to mean something improper. He shook his head and turned away, as though that had settled the matter. Moira wasn't so easily dissuaded.

"Well, she will not be left here to fend for herself. I won't stand for it. She is practically my family, all the family I have in the world at this moment. And I say she will accompany us to your home. Gretchen, put your things in Mr. MacAteer's wagon.

"Aye, my lady," Gretchen replied with a short curtsy. Pryor's eyes went wide.

"There'll be no more of that kind of talk, I won't stand for it! If she's going to follow you everywhere you go, she's to be her own person, none of this 'my lady' nonsense!" Pryor stormed away to retrieve Gretchen's things for her, his disposition toward her warming slightly from the realization that she was a servant and therefore had no say in her own affairs. Both ladies had been taken aback by his lashing out, but neither spoke a word against it.

The ride to Pryor's cabin had been just as tense, and very little was said throughout the long trip. Once Moira had tried to speak to Gretchen, reverting to Irish so as not to make the harsh man aware of her words, but Gretchen only shook her head, afraid of the wrath that talking about him could arise. Speaking Irish had long been outlawed back home anyway, despite the old Lord Brennan's insistence that it be taught and spoken in his household; but this was certainly not Brennan Castle, and it wouldn't do to be caught speaking the forbidden language in unfamiliar territory, and with unfamiliar people about.

Now, as they set to work with a fervor, the bargain in exchange for lodging until the whole situation could be understood, they took the chance to learn their surroundings, to see the first real glimpse of open sky such as they'd not seen since stepping aboard the ship back in Ireland.

"Hey there! You... um, ladies," a hesitant voice called out while they worked in the barn. "Supper's ready!" Moira and Gretchen peeked out of the barn and saw Pryor standing on the porch of the cabin, a ladle in his hand. Together, they hoisted the nearly full pail of milk to the shelf, then closed the barn door firmly behind them and crossed the pasture to the house, the smell of something cooking growing stronger as they approached.

Inside the cabin, both ladies were taken by surprise for

the hundredth time that day. Neither had seen the interior of the handsomely built cabin until that moment. Rather than a ruffian's shack filled with items thrown haphazardly in corners and tossed askew on the floor, the inside of the cabin had been outfitted for a wife and a family. The outside of the cabin led to the impression that the floors would be bare earth, but it was instead made from hand-cut boards that had been sanded to almost silky softness. Rather than one room that served every purpose, they could now see there were at least three rooms: a large room that served as a gathering area, eating nook, and kitchen, and then two smaller rooms off to the sides, their doors open invitingly. In the kitchen, a calico tablecloth—the fabric reclaimed from a feed sack, to be sure, but dainty and clean nonetheless— covered the hand-hewn table, while delicate curtains fluttered in front of the open windows. Dishes had been set on the table, and not just tin plates but real porcelain. It was far from fancy and nothing like the table Moira was accustomed to, but the effort involved was very real, and very much appreciated.

"Sit," he commanded not unkindly, but without any kind of warmth in his voice. "Eat."

Moira and Gretchen looked about for a basin and pitcher to wash their hands, but finding none, stepped back outside to the well that Pryor had dug. They hauled up a bucket of icy water, the wind whipping the moisture on their hands until they turned red and shook. They returned to the cabin with their arms around each other for warmth, but also for comfort at having to face this stranger in his home.

The dinner itself, however, was a more unpleasant experience than the company they were forced to keep. Pryor's attempts at serving beans and cornbread resulted in a congealed mass of cornmeal mush, dotted here and there with beans that were hard as rocks. Both ladies tried their best to overlook the fiasco and choke down their host's food, but eventually, they gave up.

"Tell me, Mr. MacAteer, did you soak these beans long before attempting to cook them?" Moira asked in what she hoped was a kindly, non-judgmental tone.

"Soak them? Why?"

"Because it makes them turn soft when they're cooking. Dried beans should be allowed to soak for several hours. Overnight, if possible." Gretchen nodded enthusiastically before using the tip of her spoon to scrape together another bite of mush that didn't contain the hearty pebbles.

"Oh. I wondered how other people got 'em to taste like that. I didn't know about that step."

"Well, there should be a recipe in that cookbook up there…" Moira began, but stopped herself when she saw the cautious look on the man's face. She instantly overcame her faux pas by suddenly turning on Gretchen, admonishing the young girl for having her elbows dangerously close to the table's edge, looking very much like she might place them there. For her part, the maid looked confused at the chastising, but when Moira grabbed her hand beneath the table and gave it a light squeeze, she returned her mistress' smile. Moira inclined her head ever so slightly at the man seated with them, and Gretchen understood immediately.

Pryor looked on at their exchange, perplexed at why anyone would care where someone's elbows happened to fall. He did sit up straighter though, moving his own elbows aside to make sure they didn't offend.

"So, Mr. MacAteer, why don't you tell me about how you came to be in Montana?" Moira asked, hoping for more information on the man, and a way to deflect attention from her earlier slip. Pryor just shook his head.

"Nothing to tell, and please don't call me Mr. MacAteer anymore. The name's Pryor, but folks just call me Pry."

"Pry, then," Moira agreed in an overly chipper voice. "Surely there must be some story behind your journey to the West, your wishes to set up a life out here on your own."

"Nothing to tell. But what about you? Surely there must be a story there of your own to worry about?" His response wasn't unkind, but it certainly lacked any semblance of cordiality. Moira chose to take the higher road and answer him, ignoring his brusque tone and measuring her responses carefully.

"I chose to come to America to avoid controversy within my family," she began, choosing her words carefully lest he take the wrong impression of her.

"Let me guess. Your dad was forcing you to marry some disgusting old codger just because he had money?" Pryor asked ruefully.

"My father has passed away. My mother, too, before you say something disrespectful about her as well." She waited while Pryor mumbled an apology, looking down at his half-eaten meal. "But to answer your question, yes, marriage to a disgusting old codger—a wealthy one, even—was almost unavoidable. And my brother's life was in jeopardy if I refused to marry him; therefore, I removed myself from the scenario."

Pryor looked at Moira for a moment with newfound respect. "So you stowed away on a ship and came all this way? I have to say it, I am impressed. That took ingenuity, but it also took more courage than most men I know even have in them."

"First of all, Mister MacA—I mean, Pryor," she began, correcting herself when she saw the faint look of warning on his face. "I did not stow away. I not only have too much class and good breeding for that sort of behavior, I am also a lady of means. Therefore, I purchased our passage, as well as paid for my claim once I reached New York."

"What do you mean? You've paid your full claim?" Pryor dropped his spoon to his plate with a clatter and sat back in his chair, looking between the two women to see if this was some kind of a trick. "Most men who come out here take years of sweat and prayer to pay off what they owe, and there's already some who've lost everything and had to head back east. There's some who couldn't even afford the train passage or a passing coach to head home. They had to start back on foot carrying what was left of their belongings on their backs."

Moira looked to Gretchen to see that the younger girl wasn't frightened by the reality Pryor described, but her wide-eyed look gave her away. The maid, although certainly not a girl of any kind of her own wealth, had always been aligned to the Brennan's household and had therefore never felt the pinch of want, especially not where sustenance and basic comforts of life were concerned. Moira gave her maid a reassuring smile before turning back to Pryor.

"Well, fortunately, that is not the circumstance I find myself in. As a matter of fact, I need to begin acquiring supplies of my own very soon if I'm to begin developing my land."

Pryor regarded her again silently, watching her for a moment as he weighed his words. His solemn expression grew somewhat darker.

"Your land? You thinking of building on your claim? But what about our contract?"

CHAPTER EIGHT

"**W**hat of it? I have already stated to you quite plainly that I did not enter into any contract, certainly not one to be married to a complete stranger. If that was an option I could stomach, I could have stayed in Ireland and become a duchess in the bargain. I traveled all this way in search of freedom, and to keep my brother safe from harm."

Moira softened her tone at the look of obvious disappointment on Pryor's face.

"We will go through the papers together and uncover where the error lies," she continued. "If it shows that I am at fault in this misunderstanding, I will gladly repay you any costs you've incurred. As it stands, I will also happily compensate you fairly in both work and funds for your continued hospitality, if that's agreeable to you."

Pryor stood up after pondering her pronouncement. He silently cleared the dishes and placed them on the sideboard, saving the leftovers in a scrap pail for the animals. Only after he finished cleaning up from the meal did he come back to the table, standing over his chair as he said, "I didn't think this arrangement was just hospitality. I hoped you were agreeing to come with me."

"I'm sorry you were mistaken," Moira said in a soft voice, barely above a whisper. "Let us see where the confusion occurred, and then we can set about trying to write off for a new wife for you, one who is eager to meet you, as I'm sure there are plenty of women wont to do. You are a generous and honorable man, and I know there must be no shortage of able women who would be proud to become your wife."

Pryor nodded thoughtfully then sat down. Moira breathed a sigh of relief at his acceptance of the situation, then, with a nod and a spoken word of thanks, dismissed Gretchen. The maid retreated to a chair in the corner of the living area and retrieved her knitting from her bag, her sure sign that she was dutifully no longer participating in her mistress' conversation. Pryor watched the exchange, but was more bemused than irritated by it this time.

"Does she always do what you say?" he asked with a cocky smirk. "Can't she do anything for herself?"

"I'm not sure why that disturbs you. She was my ladies' maid back in Ireland, why should she suddenly find herself without employment just because our address has changed?"

"I don't know, I guess it makes sense when you say it that way. But there's a whole part of the country where these so-called 'servants' of yours don't have any say in the matter, and it's got a lot of people up in arms."

"I am aware of the news from the American South, and I think you must know before you let me stay on at your property that I agree completely with the abolitionists. But

Gretchen is not in those poor souls' same situation, as she has every right to come and go as she pleases. I think you'll find the situation you're describing is far different. But for now, let's look to these papers we each possess." Moira reached for the tied packet of papers Pryor had retrieved from his wall cupboard, and held it along with the telegram he'd received in the post. The telegram, which was only received in Ohio, then had to be sent by mail, which Pryor had had to pick up from the nearest military post. New Hope had no official post office, as its postmaster only took and received letters for payment of their transit, which he arranged himself at both his own cost and his own risk. It explained how the document had reached him before she did, but only by a little.

"Here is the first area of concern, Pry. This is not my signature. Look," she explained, turning the paper around to show him the papers he'd received in the post, compared to the homestead claim she'd signed in New York for Mr. Walsh. He seemed to look at them and compare them, but he only shrugged.

"I don't know enough about signatures to know what's right or wrong. But if you say they're not the same, I believe you."

"Thank you. But that's not all. This document that you received has the wrong initial right here." She pointed to the offending letter. "I have several names, as I'm the only daughter in the family and I'm named after several persons. Therefore, I don't use any single initial with my name and signature. But whomever forged this document used my first letter, D. Also, if you'll notice, my title is missing. I try my best not to count myself higher in human worth than those around me, but I am a titled young lady and therefore, I sign my documents as such. It's required of nobility, especially when entering into a contract, but this individual did not put down my title."

Pryor creased his brow as he compared the two. Even he could see that there was an irregularity to the documents, but he had no idea how or why it could have happened.

"Who would have sent me a false letter? What would anyone get out of it?" he asked, still scanning both papers.

"Money, perhaps? Is it likely you were swindled out of the fees?"

"It's possible, I suppose. But you're here, so I don't see how it could be just about money. If someone was just going to steal from me, why bother going to the trouble to sign it and arrange to send you? If I didn't know any better, I'd say this has something to do with you. I just happened to be the good excuse to get you sent out here."

"But I chose to come! I don't see how this could have happened either. Who would profit in any way from convincing me that I owned a claim, for which I have the paperwork in my hand, but then have me become your wife upon my arrival?"

"How did you say you got here?" Pryor asked, then waited patiently for Moira to explain it all in greater detail, nodding thoughtfully as he listened. "So, your brother wrote to the land office? How did he know where you would be heading if you left in the middle of the night?"

It was Moira's turn to stare pensively, mulling over the turn of events. Ronan couldn't have known her plans until he found the letter she'd left him, yet he'd been able to send a letter ahead of her? The ship that carried her had docked in a number of ports to take on passengers and cargo, so she'd just assumed a letter from Ireland had reached New York ahead of her. But Pryor was right, she'd only ever spoken to one cousin about the homestead idea. This cousin...

"My uncle!" she cried, looking aghast. The sound of her mistress' distress brought Gretchen running to Moira's side, and she cast a look at Pryor as if daring him to tell her to get back. Moira collapsed against Gretchen's shoulder, but continued. "My uncle must have learned of my plans from his son, my cousin, Francis, and then all but sold me into marriage! It was his effort to get me out of my brother's household in order to take control of the estate our father left!"

Gretchen pulled a handkerchief from her sleeve and offered it to Moira to dry her tears. Pryor, unused to ladies' emotions, leaned away from them as they clung to each other, but understood the pain Moira was suffering. He waited for her to compose herself, thinking through the strange situation they all found themselves in.

Finally, Moira's sobs quieted and she let herself be comforted in Gretchen's embrace. She moaned softly in her fear for her brother, the brother she'd left behind to face the plotting, conniving relatives and their insatiable greed. Pryor finally spoke.

"I see it now. You were tricked into coming here. You can stay until the train comes next month, and I'll return you to New Hope. Then you can go anywhere you like. There's no contract between us."

CHAPTER NINE

No matter how hard Moira protested, no matter how long Gretchen wrung her hands, Pryor would not be persuaded to let them take the barn to sleep in. He insisted on arranging a few blankets across the hay in the loft, leaving the ladies to share the bed in the safety of the cabin.

"Because there's no contract and I release you from any agreement, I guess now that makes you my guests. And what kind of host lets his guests sleep above his cows in a drafty barn? And in the dead of winter, too? It will be fine. Just be sure to pull the latch string in to keep out any intruders."

"Intruders? We're the only humans alive for hundreds of miles, are we not? We should be far safer than any other people in all of Montana!" Moira laughed gratefully.

"That's not true, I'm afraid. There are outlaws in these parts, more animal than men, and the treaties the government inflicted on the Indians aren't worth the paper they're written on. Just keep the door latched; I'll wake you after the chores are done in the morning. Good night, ladies." He nodded his head respectfully and stepped down the cabin's steps, walking toward the barn in the pitch blackness, easily tracing the path his feet had worn from his daily work.

Moira and Gretchen collapsed into the bed, but only after Moira could convince her young maid that they could share it.

"I'll not have you sleep on the floor simply because of your station. It's as Mr. MacAteer said, this is a new world, and your position back in Brennan has no bearing on where you sleep in the Montana territory. Besides, you'll catch your death of cold on the floor, and we'll both be warmer sharing the covers. Now lie down and get your first good night's rest in weeks! I command it!" she added with a proud smirk.

"Are you dismissing me from your service, my lady?" Gretchen asked, a look of horror and hurt crossing her face.

"Of course not, you've always been loyal and a source of great comfort to me! But there's nothing about your station that requires you to sleep on the floor, certainly not when we're both in such wretched circumstances, and even more, it's not because you're of a lower position. No, we'll share the bed Mr. MacAteer has been kind of enough to give us leave to enjoy."

"He is a strange man, is he not, ma'am?" Gretchen asked, slowly arranging the bedcovers and then retrieving their nightclothes from their cases. She helped Moira unpin her long hair, reserving all the pins in her apron pocket for the following morning's keeping. Next, she took the brush and began the task of caring for Moira's waist-length brown hair, combing out each curl before wrapping it smartly on a strip of cloth and tying it in place.

"That he is, though I'm certain it's not polite of us to say so in his house. Still, he has taken the news that I'm not to become his wife far better than most men. And to let us remain here instead of turning us out, he must be a kindly person."

"Tis a far better man than I would have expected, taking us in when we were in need, especially after knowing he was to be disappointed in love."

"Oh, Gretchen, remember that marriage among most in society is not about love. Take me, for instance, and that horrid Macomby. Any match made there would be about securing the future of our respective estates and ensuring an heir in the family line. Nothing more. Except in Macomby's instance, there was also his vile, lecherous nature to tolerate... I mean, of all things holy, the man already has three sons! What does he need with a wife who could bear him more children?" Moira pressed a hand delicately to her mouth, holding back her disgust at the thought.

"But Mr. MacAteer is no Lord Macomby," Gretchen replied. "He seems a decent enough man, and in possession of a goodly heart. He should have no trouble finding a caring wife if he only went a-looking. Surely he could leave his farm for a few months to meet a bride? Why fetch after a woman he's never before laid eyes on through an advertisement in a city daily?"

"You should know as well as I that there is no day when a farm can tend itself, just as a castle cannot tend to itself. Besides, Mr. MacAteer also wasn't marrying for love. Much like any lord, he had needs in the way of a helpmate for his farm and a wife to provide him children. He will need heirs to leave his hard-won land to, as much as he will need those heirs to relieve him of some of the workload of maintaining his farm. His wife and any daughters will run his household, while he and his sons will work his land. Love is of no import, but fondness that may grow over time would be welcome and expected."

"Pardon my saying so, but I never thought I'd find the one cause where being a lowly maid would bring more happiness, more... choice."

Moira smiled at her maid's observation. "You just might be right, so be sure you choose your own husband wisely! You'll have no one making a sound match for you, unless you would trust me with the task!"

"Oh, I would that I were worthy of your troubles, my lady," Gretchen teased with a curtsy. "But alas, I am destined to be a spinster and live out my days in your service."

Moira turned in her chair and took Gretchen's hands in her own to look intently in the young woman's eyes. "Do you really think so? Because it is not what I want for you." Gretchen looked pale, but before she could protest, Moira went on. "We're not in Brennan, and I don't think we ever shall be again. Back at home, I could have envisioned you happy in my household, delighted to have you choose a husband from among my other household staff. But here... there are nothing but choices here. You will always have a place with me, for as long as you wish to remain in my employ, but should the right man with the right heart find you, then you must choose a future filled with happiness and fulfilment, with a home and children of your own. Promise me you will."

"I never will, my lady! I can naw promise to leave you, and you can naw ask me to!" the maid cried. Moira only shook her head and smiled, while Gretchen returned to her work of helping her prepare for bed.

The following morning, both ladies were roused from

their sleep by a shrieking sound, the sound of animals being turned out of the barn before the sun was up over the trees. The howls and general ruckus jolted them both upright in the bed, confused about where they were for a moment. When the memory of it all came rushing back, they fell back against the pillows at the same time, giggling at their mirrored actions. Moira reached to the window and flicked back the curtain, but yelled out when she saw Pryor walking past. She clutched the bed covers and pulled them up to her chin, ducking low in the bed.

"Did he see us, ma'am?" Gretchen asked fearfully, ducking even lower than her mistress. "Me mother would have me whipped for putting me-self such on display!"

"I don't think he saw anything of importance. And something tells me he would be just as embarrassed as we are to find us without our clothes. Pay it no mind, but let us dress before it should happen again."

"You stay, my lady, I will get up. 'Tis mostly still dark outside. I will begin breakfast and rouse you when the meal is ready."

"I don't think Pryor would take kindly to me taking my tray in bed. Remember, this isn't—"

"I know, I know! This isn't Brennan," the maid interrupted morosely. "You keep reminding me that this land is naw yet our home. Pray, ma'am… where is home then? Where will we be that I can go back to my duties and not worry about offending someone's sensibilities? I am a servant, and I shall serve ye."

Gretchen cast an apologetic look for her outburst, then closed the bedroom door behind her as she went to prepare breakfast. Moira stayed put, duly chastised for not acknowledging her maid's place. But it begged the question in her own mind: where was home now?

Moira had a sudden burst of inspiration. She threw off the covers and helped herself into a clean but simple dress from her trunk, then pulled on layers of stockings and simple petticoats to keep herself warm. She had no idea what to do to make her hair meet the style Gretchen always arranged for her, but that didn't matter out here on the frontier. She was all thumbs at trying to accomplish anything more intricate than simply pulling it all back in a loose ribbon, but it would have to do. Besides, the purpose was for function, not for fashion anymore.

"Gretchen! Move aside! I am a woman in the wilds of Montana, and I am here to work!" she announced with a humorous flourish. Her maid was too surprised to argue, but instead, stood still, mouth agape, as Moira reached for the eggs Gretchen had just brought in and began cracking them clumsily into the bowl on the counter. "Like this, yes?"

Gretchen nodded, and proceeded to show her mistress how to beat the eggs with a splash of fresh milk and pour the mixture onto the hot iron skillet. Next, Gretchen began mixing the ingredients for cornbread cakes, demonstrating to Moira how to pour and then flip the first ones, then leaving her to do the rest. She gave her attention to setting the table while the water boiled for coffee, peering over her shoulder nervously to monitor the lady's progress with her first attempt at cooking.

By the time the food was prepared and Moira's mess mostly cleaned up, Pryor walked past the cabin's front door and smelled aromas that hadn't appeared in his corner of the valley in a long time. He stopped and peeked inside the cabin, amazed at the sight of wonderful nourishment and a clean kitchen.

"What's all this? You don't have to wait on me, too, remember?" he asked, turning to the maid. Gretchen colored slightly and cast her eyes at Moira.

"It was my lady's doing, sir," she said quietly, forgetting herself and curtseying as she fought back a grin at Moira's proud expression.

"Your lady?" he asked, only he wasn't angry at the title. He seemed more amused than bothered, taking in the sight of Moira's proud smirk, which she tried to mask with an air of confidence, as though she'd been caring for a household every day of her life instead of for the last half hour. "I never thought I'd live to see the day that royalty cooked me breakfast!"

"Who says this is for you?" Moira shot back, but her laugh broke through her serious expression before she could convince him of the joke. She gestured to the table for Pryor to join them after he washed up.

When they finally sat down to eat, there was no conversation for the first many minutes. Just as Moira started to worry that they'd overstepped their bounds by cooking from Pryor's stored food goods, he sat back and closed his eyes, a dreamy smile on his face.

"I haven't eaten so well since I moved my camp out here," he announced, placing his hands contentedly on his stomach. Moira noticed that he seemed to be well-toned from the hard work of farm life, but that he also looked a little thin in places. Remembering his dinner from last night, it was not a surprise.

"You're quite welcome, considering it was your food!" Moira laughed. "Of course, we'd both be starving this morning if it was not for Gretchen's considerable talents in the kitchen. If not for her, we'd not only still be hungry, your cabin would probably be a smoldering pile of cinders by now!"

The maid blushed at the praise, darting her eyes back

and forth between the other two before ducking her head. "Thank you, my... ma'am."

"Last night, you took your time to look through my documents and help me make sense of this... problem," Pryor began, sitting back in his chair and letting his hearty breakfast settle. "I can return the favor. If you have your papers on your claim, I can try to explain the way of things after the evening chores are done. That is, if you still want to settle your land, and if you'll teach me how to fix my food better so I don't waste away."

"Of course, I'd love to know more about homesteading, but I thought you were planning to pack me back off on the next train?" Moira said, looking to Gretchen. "I didn't know you'd be interested in helping us stay in Montana."

"You came all this way for something, didn't you? You might as well find it."

CHAPTER TEN

They'd struck a bargain. The ladies would help Pryor by teaching him everything he needed to know to keep his house in order and to cook his meals, and he would teach them about working the land. If, by the time the train was due, they hadn't decided they could make it on their own, he would happily give them a ride to New Hope and help them find a buyer for Moira's claim. The thought of returning back east with no prospects didn't sit well with Moira, but the idea of being stranded on a plot of land without so much as a tree overhead to protect them from the rain didn't appeal to her either. They shook on the bargain and got to work.

Gretchen and Moira both spent the day in Pryor's shadow, watching carefully as he showed them different daily tasks. He wasn't overly talkative, unless he was talking about his farm. Then his advice poured forth so plentifully, they almost couldn't keep up with the information he had to offer. His work that day took him from barn to pasture and back again.

Throughout the first three days of work on Pryor's claim, Moira injured herself more than she ever had during her entire life in Brennan. When she wasn't being kicked by a cow, stepped on by a horse, or chased by a goat with a vicious biting problem, she was taking splinters in her hands or straining her arms to carry heavy loads. If she'd thought Mr. MacAteer would prove to be a gentleman about the work, she was mistaken.

"You're not lifting that right," he called out over his shoulder. "Bend your knees when you pick up a heavy bundle, for if you just bend over to lift it, you'll be in bed for months with a broken back."

Moira glared angrily at the back of his head as he talked. She wanted to be angry and demand that he treat her more respectfully, offering to lift or carry heavy items as she was not accustomed to lifting anything more weighty than her tea cup in the afternoons, but she scolded herself as she remembered he was only preparing her to work her very own land. For that, she should be grateful, she knew it, and she felt small inside every time he ordered her about.

It was the milking lessons, though, that tested not only her patience, but her manners.

"You're not doing it right. You're going to hurt her; no wonder she keeps trying to kick you every time you come around!" he said, laughing derisively at Moira's expense.

"Then why do I need to do this? I don't even have a cow!" she exclaimed in an angry huff.

"Because you're going to have to have a cow. How do you plan to make your food, craft cheese or cream to exchange for goods in town, and breed cattle to sell to newly arrived homesteaders? A cow in milk is an important tool out here, so you're going to have to acquire one, then milk it. If you don't, she'll dry up and be useless."

"Is that a jab at the fairer sex, *Mister* MacAteer?" she asked, reverting to his formal title to emphasize her displeasure. "I'll have you know, a lady can be plenty useful, even if she's not breeding stock."

"Sure she can... she's just even more useful if she breeds," he said, his former embarrassment at that kind of talk gone. He shot her a look that dared her to challenge him. "Pray tell, then, what use would this cow be if she didn't give milk?"

"There are plenty of things a fine animal can do. She is a reason to wake up for chores each morning, she could be a fine pet, and she could even provide meat once her time on this earth is up."

Pryor laughed openly at Moira's view of livestock. "You're gonna lose your farm if you keep animals around as pets! Every animal on the place has to contribute in some way. Look at the pigs, even. They don't provide anything except meat once they're butchered, but they work every day."

"Your pigs? You're trying to convince me that your pigs work your farm? Now who doesn't know a thing about farms?" She scoffed and tried once again to go back to the milking, but the cow was having none of it. Pryor came around to watch her efforts again.

"Of course they work. They eat the scraps, the leftover corn husks, and the bones from any game I kill. Why, if not for the pigs, I'd be sitting in a pile of my own garbage, attracting bears and other deadly animals. The pigs keep the place clean each day."

Moira relaxed her angry posture slightly. "I see. I had not considered it that way."

"That's because you're a princess who lived in a castle. But even your castle had pigs, and swineherds to tend them, otherwise, you'd have all sunk in your own filth. You should have stepped outside the walls and noticed the rest of the people once in a while, then you'd know these things."

Pryor's tone had turned biting again, and his open scorn for her station was beginning to wear on her already thin nerves. He'd made more than one reference to her wealth or station, and not in an admiring way.

"I'll have you know that I did know my people!" she cried out, knocking over the still empty milk bucket and standing up from her stool so quickly, the cow startled. Pryor startled at her outburst, too. "I knew them every one by name and by position. I tended them when they were ill or injured, and cared for their sick children as their fevers raged or the women struggled in their childbeds, just as my mother did before me! I was not a princess, thank you, but even if I had been, the people would have still loved me just as much as they do now! I cared for them, I saw to their comfort and needs, and I did it with respect and genuine Christian concern for them! You do not know me, Mr. Pryor, yet you sit in comfortable judgment over my every action, reveling in my ignorance of your rustic life. I am here to learn and to help you, but if you do not wish to instruct me without scorn, I will happily remove myself from your property!"

It was Pryor's turn to be humbled by another's judgment, and he had to admit that he had judged her—harshly, even—and had come up lacking because of his decision that she'd been spoiled and pampered. He raised his hands in a peaceful shrug, and apologized.

"You're right, I had no idea, and I'm sorry. I truly am," he clarified when Moira refused to look at him. She turned away, not in disgust at his accusations, but at her own tears. She'd thought only of herself when she left Brennan, and hadn't spared a single thought for the families she was leaving behind to fend for themselves when it came to needing compassion and care. "Hey now, there's no need to be unhappy. You were right, and I was wrong. Now don't be sore at me."

The pleading tone in his voice was almost Moira's undoing. He genuinely apologized, and she tried to return his smile.

"Fine. And I thank you for your kind words. Now show me how to milk this cow so I don't let my own animal go barren!"

She righted the overturned stool and bucket, then went to work again, much to the cow's continued dismay. Pryor leaned over, begged her pardon, then placed his hands over hers to demonstrate. She bristled at the strange man's touch, but when she saw the results of his instruction for herself, she very nearly laughed with relief.

"At last! It's finally working!" Moira exclaimed, taking over on her own to try the chore for herself. The animal settled down when it realized the torture of putting up with an inexperienced newcomer had come to an end, and stood lazily chewing a bit of hay while Moira finished the task. Pryor congratulated her on the new skill before heading back to his own chores, leaving his student more proud of her work than if she'd grown the animal herself.

CHAPTER ELEVEN

"Y̲ou'll have to put up a fence," he'd explained one day during their morning work of digging the holes for the posts that dotted the perimeter of his claim. "That's not just sound advice for your farm, it's required. You have to report so much in crops, plant a few different varieties, and fence your land. This here's one of the easiest fences you could build, seeing as how you two are ladies. But you'll need to order supplies, because you might not want to go splitting all the rails yourself."

The ground was still frozen in the early January temperatures, and not as forgiving as in the spring. Still, the fence had to go up or he risked losing his claim. He'd no sooner said those words than the axe he'd been wielding bounced backward off the log he'd intended to split, knocking him in the forehead with such force that he fell backwards. Both women jumped up from their spots in a flash and were by his side almost as soon as he'd hit the ground.

Gretchen let out a slight scream at the sight of the blood that was already flooding across Pryor's face, but Moira was in no mood for her maid's delicate manner. She went to work pulling the bandana from where it stuck out of Pryor's hip pocket, pushing against him to ease it out from beneath him then pressing it to the wound on his head.

"Pry! Are you all right?" she demanded in a concerned voice, lifting the cloth slightly before pressing against it again immediately to stop the blood that continued to flow freely from his torn skin. Beneath the pressure of her hand and the cloth, Pryor moaned in pain. "Aye, that's a good sign, he hasn't knocked himself completely stupid then."

"My lady! What must we do?" her maid cried as Moira continued to hold the pressure on his head. The blood had already soaked through the thin, worn cloth and pooled near Moira's wrist, but she continued to hold it in place.

"Run into the house and begin a pot of hot water. Find any spare cloth you can and cut it for wraps. Look about for a needle and thread in case the bleeding will not stop of its own accord. Go now, and hurry!" Moira peeked again as Gretchen took off, running for the cabin to do as she was bid. Pryor lifted a weak arm to try to push Moira's hand away, but she held the cloth against his wound firmly, pushing his hand back down.

"Hold still, Pry, you've hurt yourself. It's fairly deep, so hold until it bleeds less." She reached a lock of his dark hair out of the way, dizzying slightly when her hand came away covered in more blood.

It took ages for Gretchen to return to say that the water and bandages were ready. She'd managed to find a needle and a spool of coarse thread but had to rummage through Pryor's stash of supplies to do so, and immediately apologized.

"I'm sorry to say but there's naught to be done but that

I'll have to stitch him. I'd best not do it here though, where there's muck and mud all 'round us," Moira explained. Gretchen turned a fair shade of green at the suggestion, telling Moira all she needed to know about who was going to go about doing the unpleasant task. "I'm just not sure we can both hold him down for it. He'll have to wake slightly so we can tell him what we're doing to his poor head!"

"I found this, my lady," Gretchen said, holding out a dusty bottle of homemade liquor. It was so old, the handwriting on the label was faded, and a layer of thick grime covered it.

"Oh, Gretchen, you're brilliant! That will be a tremendous help, thank you. We'll just have to convince him to drink it up before we go needling him."

"I was thinking to cleanse the wound, ma'am," the maid answered with a light laugh. Moira joined her.

"I think we're both right! He'll need some in the wound to clean it out and prevent infection, but I dare say the stitching will go far easier on him if he finishes the rest of it! I do like the fact that there's so much whisky left in a bottle so old. It says he's not a drinking man, and Lord above knows there are plenty of those to be had here on earth."

"How will we get him to the house then?"

"Hmmm... I know. Hold this in place, I'll return shortly." Moira passed off the duty of holding pressure on the wound to her maid and ran to the barn, only to return with a wooden wheelbarrow that had seen better days. Between the two of them, they managed to roll Pryor into it, only to have the bleeding start fresh when he landed face down with his head pitched forward out of the small cart. Moira grabbed the cloth and held fast again while helping Gretchen shove the now heavy cart across the frozen ground and toward the cabin.

The porch steps proved to be another obstacle, but, by hoisting him between them across their shoulders, they were able to get him inside before dropping him on the bed. Moira took up a fresh strip of cloth and unworked his boots while Gretchen gathered everything they would need to staunch the bleeding.

"Are we ready, do you suppose?" Moira asked, holding the bottle of liquor in front of her like an offending draught of poison. Gretchen nodded, and Moira held the bottle to Pryor's slack mouth, urging him to drink. What didn't run into his mouth pooled in the rough fabric of his shirt, but at least he became conscious enough to swallow and cringe at the offending taste.

Moira pulled back the bandage and poured a small stream of the clear amber liquid into the gash on his head, closing her eyes briefly at the jagged edges of skin and what she could have sworn was bone showing clearly beneath it. She steeled herself, and bade Gretchen hold the pressure while she threaded the needle.

"Should we not give the liquor more time to work? 'Twill hurt him much, will it not?" she asked, but Moira shook her head.

"Tis only whisky and not a magic potion, I'm afraid. It will only take the edge off the pain. Nothing short of another blow to the head would make him not feel it, and I for one am not up to bashing him in the skull! Would that I had taken to the drink; it will take strength enough to stomach piercing his skin to save him."

"My lady, I think we'd best hurry. Look, he's gone white as a sheet."

Moira looked at his face and was shaken by the peacefulness in his expression, the pale look of someone who could easily slip into the grave. It strengthened her resolve for the unpleasant task of hurting him even more. She pinned his outstretched arm beneath her knee and spoke loudly in his ear.

"Pryor, do you hear me? I'm sorry, but we have to stitch. Please, I beg of you, please try to be still." She nodded to Gretchen, who pinned his other arm before sliding her hand on top of his scalp to hold his hair back, giving Moira access to the ugly wound. Moira took a deep breath and held it, willing herself not to give way to a weak stomach at a time like this. She forced herself to look closely at the gash, lining up her stitches. She pushed the end of the needle through the first layer of skin and bade herself ignore the brief cry of pain from her poor patient.

When they'd finished tending to Pryor, Moira and Gretchen cleaned up the mess of their surgery efforts and sat together at the table in the kitchen, neither one speaking much. The reality of the situation was far too great to think about. What if they'd been unable to stop the bleeding, and found themselves stranded here, unable to even find their way back to the nearest town? What if they'd never come at all, and this injury had happened when Pryor was simply out working on his land? The gravity of it all weighed on them.

"I don't know what we're to do," Moira finally whispered, looking down at her hands as though she could still see traces of Pryor's blood in the creases. Gretchen got up and came to her, standing behind her mistress and comforting her in her gentle hug. "What if we could not have saved him, what if he had died? This is all too real, Gretchen. This is not a game for children, this playing at adventure. This... makes me wonder if we would not have fared better back in Ireland."

"My lady, no. Do naw say such a thing! You, married to

that terrible man? You think that would be better than having your freedom?"

"At least there, I would know what to do if a man's life was in danger."

"But mistress, you did know what to do! You took care of him, just as your mother taught you by her knee. You're only now feeling the fear that you pushed down when you needed to be strong, that's all."

"I hope you're right, dear. But this has made me see Montana with new eyes. And Pryor..."

"Yes, my lady? What of him?" Gretchen asked, puzzled at the silence that Moira's sentence left hanging between them.

"Oh, no, that's all."

"If you'll pardon my saying so..." the maid began, but she, too, let her sentence hang unfinished for the space of a moment.

"Yes, Gretchen? You were going to say?" The maid shook her head, thinking better of her boldness. "Well, don't stop on my account! You've been doing nothing more than begging my pardon ever since we left Brennan!" Only instead of a fierce glare from the lady, Gretchen was relieved to see a hint of humor touching Moira's eyes, even if she wasn't yet ready to smile after the day they'd endured.

"I was only going to say, ma'am... you seemed... worried. For Mr. MacAteer, I mean." Gretchen immediately pressed her lips together, willing herself to keep quiet.

"Why, of course I was worried. He could have bled to death right before our eyes! It was... frightening, to say the very least!"

"I meant to say, it seemed... more."

"More?" Moira looked up at Gretchen with a confused look. Her maid nodded fervently, still pressing her mouth closed. "Pray, explain yourself?"

"You just seemed... overly concerned, that is all."

"Of course I was! I've already said that an accident to Mr. MacAteer could have been disastrous for all three of us, not the least of which is because he could have died!"

"I know, you're right, forget I spoke." Gretchen turned to wash out the dishes and cloths they'd used to work on Pryor, smiling to herself when her back was turned to her mistress. She knew what she'd seen, and it warmed her heart. Moira had been afraid of losing Pryor, and not only for the reasons she voiced aloud.

CHAPTER TWELVE

"Oh, no, you don't, you're in the bed today!" Moira called out from the kitchen table where she sat, already ready for the workday ahead of her, eating a meager breakfast while Gretchen prepared heartier fare—recuperative food, at that—for their patient. "I will handle your chores, just tell me what to do!"

Pryor eyed her suspiciously, not certain whether or not this was a joke they were playing on him, or if he was still experiencing a concussion from his slip up the day before. It could just as well have been sleep deprivation that had his mind playing tricks on him, he reasoned, as they'd taken turns waking him during the night to see that his head injury wasn't worse.

"Oh, you will, your highness? You're going to shovel out the animals' stalls, do the milking, and put up six new fence posts before dinner time? I'd like to see that!" he scoffed, his usual quiet nature replaced by the irritability brought on by the pounding in his head and the itch of the woman's needlework.

"I can guarantee the milking and the shoveling, as unpleasant as that sounds. The fence may have to wait until you're back on your feet. But surely it's been this long, a few more days won't be your ruination. Back to bed with you then, and Gretchen will bring in your breakfast shortly. Go! Go!"

Moira shuttled him back into the room, but saw a light smattering of blood on the sheets that alarmed her. She grabbed up the lamp from the kitchen table and returned with it held high, leaning closer to inspect the bloody mark and then the stitches in Pryor's head.

"Oh, thank goodness, 'tis only from your shirt!" she said with a relieved smile. "I am sorry for that, but we left you in your soiled clothes and it has stained your bedding. We'll be sure to wash it fresh today. We didn't want to move you any more than we had to; heaven knows we'd hurt you plenty during the stitching. Here, change into your nightshirt and hand out your work shirt. We'll be sure to wash it, too. Gretchen is a wonder at the laundry, I promise. And we won't look at you until it's dry and returned to your person!"

Moira was grateful for the early hour and the lack of sunlight so Pryor couldn't see the bright red blush on her cheeks. Here she stood, openly discussing undressing a man, one she'd only known for a matter of a day or two. To his credit, Pryor seemed equally flustered at the conversation, but reached to take the nightshirt as he was told. She ducked out the door and closed it firmly behind her, letting it shut with more force than necessary to secure the man who would soon be nude behind the solid oak door.

"My lady? Are you feeling well?" Gretchen asked, rushing to her and pressing her hand to Moira's pink cheek, made all the more prominent by her ordinarily creamy white complexion.

"Oh, yes, but I fear I may have just made a brazen fool of myself! I wasn't thinking, and I told him to take off his clothes!" Moira said with a shocked laugh. Gretchen stared at her with wide eyes, nearly dropping the tin of biscuits she'd taken from the Dutch oven.

"Mistress?"

"Oh, no, I don't mean it that way, don't be daft! I meant I told him to change his clothes and you or I would wash the blood from his shirt!" The young women dissolved in a fit of surprised giggles, causing Pryor to laugh quietly to himself behind the closed door, enjoying their happy sound more than he thought he would.

It had been a lonely three years for Pryor, years that had given him nothing but time to think. He occupied his days with work, providing him with a well-built and comfortable house, a small herd of five head of cattle, a secure pen where he kept a modest number of pigs, and two horses to pull his wagon and plow. All told, his hard work had allowed him to bring in three years' worth of steady, comfortable wheat and corn harvests, save what had been lost each year to locusts and storms.

What Pryor didn't set aside from his harvests for seed and for his own sustenance had been sold each season, providing him with enough funds to outfit his land with a sturdy barn, a solid plow, and other tools he would need to survive during the years that wouldn't be so kind on the frontier. He'd built a smokehouse to cure meats and a strong room above it to store his food for the winter months when game would be scarce, then spent the spring months when the ground was soft digging a root cellar to store vegetables from the garden beside the barn. He'd even had time and resources to build a strong, high fenced-in pasture to turn his animals out for fresh air without fear that he'd lose his livestock to bears or panthers, both of which were plentiful in the region.

He was a man who'd been greatly blessed in his years on his claim, and he was painfully aware that all he'd built with his own two hands and intelligence could be taken away in an instant. A storm that leveled his property, a swarm of pests that decimated his crop and left him broke at year's end, or even an illness or injury that prevented him from working would destroy everything he'd worked for.

And a day of rest for something as silly as a cut to the forehead wouldn't be enough to put him to bed, not when there were chores to done and a fence line to finish before the deadline. Homesteaders only had a set amount of time to finish their obligations on their claims, and it was only a matter of months before his date came due. Pryor had had the foresight to begin his fence at the farthest points from his house and work his way home, meaning these last few acres left to be secured were nearby. He'd originally done it to keep any future neighbors from "accidentally" absorbing his property into their own, but now it meant that he no longer had a day's ride to go work on his fence. The months of riding to fence work, spending weeks at a time sleeping on the bare ground in the unprotected wide open land, were months he couldn't plant or grow his livestock because he wouldn't be near enough to tend to them.

"I'm ready to get to work," Pryor announced, emerging from the bedroom with his clean nightshirt tucked into his denim overalls. Both ladies stared in horror for a second before remembering their manners and turning away. "What? I made this shirt from almost identical cloth as the work shirt you're holding. Why is one acceptable for ladies' eyes, and the other scandalous? It's just as decent, now come on, we have work to do."

"You're right, Pry," Moira said, forcing her voice to remain steady in the presence of a man in his night clothes. "There's work to be done, and lessons to be learned about working my claim. But first, you have to have a good meal, and then, you have to agree to not overexert yourself today. There's no better way to learn than by doing, and I ask that you sit yourself beside us and instruct us in your chores. I don't want to have to repeat my embroidery when you snap the threads holding your head together!"

Pryor laughed, instinctively touching the bandage tied around his head. "Believe me, I don't want any more of your stitching, either, not that I'm not grateful to you for doing it. I never thanked you for having the steely gumption to bring me in the house and fix me up, by the way. So, thank you... thank you both."

"You're quite welcome, although I truly hope never to have to do that again," Moira answered. Behind her, Gretchen nodded eagerly, the memory of the incident obviously paining her.

They finished their food in relative silence, other than a few questions from Pryor about how the food had been cooked, making mental notes to remember how to mix ingredients and add flavorings. Gretchen turned the talk to the need for Pryor to rend some of the fat for cooking and baking the next time he slaughtered a pig, which turned the talk to a lively conversation of their favorite childhood foods. Pryor was surprised to know that many of Moira's and Gretchen's fond memories of their favorite foods from Brennan were meals Pryor had had at his grandmother's own table.

"She was from Cork," he explained with a happy expression, remembering Christmases in his grandparents' cabin in Ohio. He wore an almost dreamy look as he remembered the holidays filled with family members and the mixture of Irish and English on his mother's side, and French and English from his father's relatives.

"So how did you come to be here if all of your family are far away?" Moira asked, genuinely interested in knowing what would make a man move away from home and live an isolated, solitary existence.

"I think I've asked you the same thing," he said with a rueful grin.

"And I believe I've answered you!" she retorted playfully. "So now it is your turn. Why come all this way and live the life of a monk?"

Pryor shrugged. "Just looking for adventure, I suppose. With my family long gone—I lost my parents to influenza, and my sisters are married and living far away—there was nothing keeping me there. When I found the notices posted offering land to all comers, I decided it was time to see this frontier that so many people were talking about."

Moira smiled and was about to open her mouth to respond when she looked around and saw that Gretchen wasn't in sight. She finally spotted the maid in the bedroom, removing the blood-stained linens for the washing. Gretchen looked up, as if she sensed her mistress watching her, and gave Moira a knowing look. She grinned with delight and cocked her head in Pryor's direction.

That little sneak! Leaving the room so the two of us could talk! Has she forgotten why we're in this barren territory in the first place? Moira thought, seething only a little at her maid's innocent view of romance. *Oh, Gretchen, my dear, if only it was as simple as you make it seem.*

Moira was now, for the first time in her life, a woman of property. All that she'd endured to get here, nay, all that they'd endured together, would be for nothing if Moira married. Her husband would control everything, even here in America, this famed land of opportunity. And she'd hadn't come all this way to see that happen.

The three of them headed out, Pryor and Moira to tend to the animals and work on the fence, and Gretchen to the creek some half mile away to do the washing, despite the cold air and the sure to be frozen water. She gathered a basket of clothes and kitchen rags and set out, following the direction Pryor pointed.

"Is it safe?" Moira asked, staring fearfully after her maid. "There are no dangers out here? No wild animals? No men who would do her harm?"

"There shouldn't be any animals at this time of day, least ways not the ones what would be big enough to hurt a full-grown girl. As for men? They'd be awfully foolish to come onto another man's property, and the creek is a full fifty acres into my land."

Moira watched after Gretchen, finally turning away reluctantly and following Pryor to the barn. True to his word, he let Moira tend to the animals while he kept a respectful distance, only chuckling to himself at her mistakes and outright blunders once or twice. His horse was hesitant about this strange woman on the property, but he was quickly won over when Moira produced a carrot from her pocket, pinched from Pryor's root cellar for the very purpose of winning over a strange horse.

"They were my horse's favorite," she explained, turning to speak to Pryor over her shoulder and laughing out loud when the horse took advantage of her distraction to nose her pocket for another carrot.

"Did you ride much back in Ireland?" he asked, reaching out to pet the horse's flank while Moira pressed her cheek lovingly to the soft velvet of its chestnut brown nose.

"Oh, aye, nearly every day. Father would stage elaborate fox hunts for his associates and we would sometimes be gone all day. It was wonderful, not the hunting part so much, but the riding out of doors and the feeling of flying as my horse galloped through the hills. Of course, there is not much for a high born lady to do out of doors except ride her horse. We're far too delicate in our natures for anything more demanding," she replied sarcastically, pressing a hand to her heart and fluttering her eyelashes.

Pryor laughed, but even he could hear the truth that Moira hadn't spoken aloud: this freedom to make choices that she'd spoken of wasn't only about avoiding a marriage. It was about casting off the expectations society placed on her, and unlocking herself from the invisible chains that had held her throughout her entire life. He was surprised to find there was an unexpected need in him to help her find that freedom, no matter what it cost him.

CHAPTER THIRTEEN

That night, both Moira and Gretchen collapsed in bed from exhaustion, grateful to not have to sleep at the table as they had the night before. Pryor's injury, though still an angry-looking gash, was not so severe that he couldn't get a good night's rest, such as it would be back in the barn. They were too weary to argue when he insisted they return to their room in the cabin, and instead, waved gratefully before locking the door for the night.

"I did not think to ask you how the washing went, although I can tell it must have been fine as these linens smell fresh!" Moira said, pulling the covers up and sighing contentedly. With the winter air so frigid, the maid had had to hang them over the woodstove to force them to dry, and the homey smell of smoke combined with the washing soap lulled Moira into a warm embrace of comfort. Gretchen giggled softly, the tiredness in her voice coloring her happiness.

"Oh, I nearly forgot! There was a man passing by the

creek when I was at the washing!" she exclaimed. Moira sat up in alarm.

"What? And you didn't think to say something sooner?"

"I'm sorry, my lady, I got distracted when I returned," she answered, referring to the work of sorting through Pryor's dry goods then replacing the ticking in the mattress with a new pile of hay from the barn. She'd ended her day with washing all the floors, even the porch, before helping to see to the evening chores with her mistress.

"Oh, I apologize, Gretchen, that's not how I meant to speak. I only meant to say that there should not have been anyone nearby; Pryor told me thus. The creek runs through his property, and anyone who comes this way has had to step onto his land. Forgive me, I didn't mean to imply that you'd done anything wrong."

"No, I understand, miss. But this man was no stranger. He said he knows Mr. MacAteer, although he kept calling him Mac. He wanted me to tell him that he's returned to Montana. Could it be someone who had a land claim and had to abandon it, like Mr. MacAteer told us?"

"Anything is possible, I dare say," Moira replied, laying back against the pillows and letting herself relax once more. "We must remember to let Pryor know first thing in the morning, in case these two gentlemen have business to conduct together."

"Aye, ma'am," Gretchen mumbled before yawning widely. "If I can remember that far off…"

Fortunately, Moira reminded her in the morning, and Gretchen ducked her head shyly as she addressed Pryor over another filling breakfast.

"There was a gentleman at the creek yesterday who said he wished to see you, but he neglected to give me his name," she began, watching Pryor's face to make sure he wasn't angered by the news. "A tall man, on a grey horse, a very sad-looking animal, if I may say so."

"Yes, you may say so!" Pryor answered with a shout. "That sounds like Nathaniel Russell! Was he about this tall, with bright yellow hair?" Gretchen looked to Moira for approval before nodding, but Moira only cocked her head to the side and waited for the girl to finish. "I'll be damn— I mean, I'm certainly surprised he's back!"

Both ladies blushed and stood immobile at the coarse language, which only made Pryor laugh. "While you're learning to milk a cow and build a fence, you might need to learn to accept a few phrases in this American language! I'm sure by the time you've hit yourself in the thumb for the hundredth time, you won't be too proud to yell a few of these words yourself!"

They eventually laughed, and Gretchen continued. "He says he'd like to come 'round and pay you a visit, now that he's to be back on his property."

"Did something ill befall Mr. Russell?" Moira asked, trying not to be nosy about others in the area, but wondering what could cause a fellow homesteader to be forced to leave his land.

"You could say that. As you know, you don't get to choose your claim. It's given to you by random selection. His happens to be on some fairly rocky soil, and with only a small portion of a creek running through it, one that stayed dry during the summer months when water was already scarce. He lost everything he had after two bad harvests, and had to look for work elsewhere. Lucky for him, the railroad came through this region and he signed on. It's dangerous work, and I'm glad to hear that he survived. If he's back, he must have earned enough money to stay on for another year."

"How far away is his land that his soil is so very different from your own?"

"Not far at all, actually. His property neighbors mine. His just slopes up toward the hills some, so it's filled with rocks that made plowing and planting too hard. I tried to help him out a little by offering to share my fence line with him so that at least one side of his property would be accounted for, but he wouldn't hear of it. Thought it was charity, or so he said. Anyway, last I heard from him, he was taking that railroad job. I'm not much of a church-going man, but I'm not ashamed to say I found myself praying for old Nathaniel more than once."

"That doesn't seem fair at all! How can they take his money and allot him a portion of land that cannot be farmed?" Moira cried, indignant for the man who'd lost so much that he'd had to risk his life just to keep from losing more.

"It's the way of it. Settling land is a gamble, just as sure as throwing down your money in a game of cards. 'Course, farming is a gamble anyway. You have to have faith that there will be plenty of water and no hail storms, and that your animals won't take sick or lame. Even if everything goes your way, you're gambling that the price of your harvest will be enough to feed you for another year. At least when you gamble, you have a chance that things will turn out all right. For some of these fellas, and for a lady or two I know, having any kind of small chance was more chance than they'd ever had."

"That was quite poetic, Pryor," Moira said, a new respect for the man evident in her voice. He looked up from his breakfast and caught her watching him, then smiled sheepishly when he realized there was no hint of ridicule in her expression. He nodded, then went back to his breakfast.

Their early morning meal carried them through another long, back breaking day. Gretchen carried out her household chores while Moira learned more about running her claim from Pryor. After the midday meal was done and the dishes washed, it was Gretchen's turn to learn more about tending the animals while Moira demonstrated, looking at Pryor from time to time to make sure she was doing it right.

"When will it ever become intuitive?" Moira asked as they walked back to the fields afterward.

"What do you mean?" Pryor asked, cocking his head and looking at her sideways.

"I mean, when will the day come that I'll just know what needs to be done, and know how to do it? When do I begin to know what a sky is going to do later in the day just by looking out my window over a morning cup of coffee? When do know that a horse has a rock in his shoe just by the way he's tossing his head? You know these things, just as surely as if someone whispered them in your ear. How does that kind of knowledge of the land happen?"

"I don't rightly know," he answered after a long pause. "It's something that just happens, probably from knowing that you have to know these things to survive out here, not just to do well. If you're caught out on your property in a storm, you could be hurt or killed. If your horse becomes lame from an untended hoof, you're not plowing or harvesting, and you're not driving into town for supplies or for a doctor. You start to notice the things that matter and make a difference, and pay better attention to them than to the things that don't seem to matter so much anymore."

Moira listened intently, wondering which things mattered now and which ones weren't so important anymore. In just the few days she'd been in Montana, and the months she'd spent getting to America and then getting to the frontier, some of the things that once drove her back in Brennan—the business affairs, the appearances to keep up for other nobles, the parties and dinners—were almost laughable. She had crossed a raging ocean and crossed a vast country, all to be allowed to make her own decisions. She would learn to separate the vital from the unnecessary, because her success here wasn't just a matter of life and death, but of freedom versus bondage, versus death for her brother.

"There are times during the day when I'm not sure I made a wise decision," she said quietly. Pryor didn't respond, as he had no words of comfort to convince her. Able-bodied men who'd worked the land since they could stand up on their own legs had failed out here, and this woman, a pampered lady who'd never lifted her own ladle before arriving in Montana, hoped to make a living on her own. He had nothing to encourage her with.

"It's worse at night, just before I go to sleep," she continued as they walked. "That's when I remember that if something happened to me, my brother would never know it. Worse, I've put poor Gretchen in harm's way. If something happens to her, if she takes ill or is hurt like you were, there would be no one to blame but me for her fate. I would never forgive myself."

"It's not as bad as all that," Pryor finally promised her. "Sure, it's hard living out here, but you have a good head on your shoulders and you're determined. You know that I'll help you in any way I can…" He left his sentence hanging between them, suddenly aware of what those words meant to him.

The air around Pryor seemed to turn thin as he realized what he was really hearing: Moira might give up and head home. She'd only just arrived, but had already seen that this life might be more than she had signed up for. Her thoughts were back home in Ireland, where everything she knew was familiar even if it wasn't perfect.

He couldn't explain the tugging feeling he felt in his chest, the desperate need to say something to convince her she could be successful with a farm of her own. What had happened in just the last few days to make him so determined to have her stay? Was it the hope he'd let himself feel when he received his papers stating that a wife was on the way? The hope that came from knowing he wouldn't be alone anymore? His farm was thriving where others' farms had failed, but it meant nothing if every day, he woke up to an empty house and every night, he went to sleep in an empty bed.

Rather than explain his feelings, his desperate sense that he couldn't bear for her to leave, he forced a bright smile onto his face and turned to speak.

"I know exactly what you need! We need to see your land, see what you have to work with. Then we need to make a trip into New Hope for supplies. Once you see your very own land and you have the supplies to work it, you'll feel better. I know you will."

CHAPTER FOURTEEN

After the early chores the following morning, Pryor hitched his team of horses to his wagons and spread a fresh pile of hay in the wagon box, both for the horses to eat during the day and for the ladies to sit on as they traveled. Gretchen packed a large wicker basket with food and glass jars of fresh water from the creek, and Moira made sure she brought the map to her very own claim.

They'd gone through the papers the night before, sitting all together at Pryor's table with the glow of an oil lamp bathing the room in flickering yellow light. He traced the lines of the map with a worn-smooth fingertip, calling out specific landmarks in the landscape, nothing more than rocks or trees or small mountains that meant nothing to Moira yet. Gretchen looked on with interest for only a few moments, but retired to her knitting, a habit that was increasingly odd to Moira. What was her maid's determination to constantly remove herself from the room when Pryor spoke to Moira? In Brennan, Gretchen had always been seated nearby, usually away from the center of attention but always readily available to keep Moira company or provide a distraction for her at a particularly boring event. But here, every time Moira looked to her, Gretchen was leaving her alone with Pryor, as though she worked against some matchmaking agenda.

"Why do you do that?" Moira asked her maid as they got ready for bed, Pryor having safely rolled up Moira's documents and returned them to her before retiring to the barn again.

"Do what, my lady?" Gretchen asked coyly, but it wasn't long before the sly smile she'd been attempting to hold back broke out, the corners of her mouth pulling back devilishly, no matter how hard she tried to keep a straight face.

"You know good and well what I mean! Any time Mr. MacAteer so much as glances in my direction, you turn and leave the room! I don't know what your motives are, dear, but I'm on to you!" Moira had meant for her scolding to be stern, or at least serious, but instead, she found herself nearly laughing at her maid's innocent expression.

"But I don't know what you mean, ma'am! I'm merely going about my duties. I'm sorry that there are naw more servants about to keep me free to stay by you, as there had been in Brennan Castle, but I'll just have to make do!" Gretchen was very nearly laughing as she tried to defend herself, which only made Moira press the subject even further.

"Tell me true, Gretchen, are you leaving us alone on purpose?"

The maid stopped laughing, and instead, gave her mistress a comforting smile. "Is that what you think, ma'am?" Moira nodded, pursing her lips to keep from reprimanding the girl. "If you think I'm leaving you alone with Mr. MacAteer, then you must have a reason to think so. Is it possibly because you fancy him?"

Moira's eyes grew wide and she opened her mouth to protest. Her maid had no right to speak to her that way. But instead of looking sheepish or chastised, Gretchen had the nerve to raise an eyebrow and give her mistress a knowing look.

"Are you being impish with me?" Moira demanded, throwing her hand on her hip in a callous manner, more surprised than angry at her maid's boldness. Gretchen only giggled again.

"So what if I am? Are you going to put me aside and find a new ladies' maid?" She laughed out loud again when Moira looked horrified at the thought. "I dare not think you'd find anyone out here to do up your hair and your buttons! But to answer your question, my lady, yes... I'm leaving the two of you alone by design."

"And why is that, pray you?"

"Because he's a good man, and just as you cannaw find another lady's maid, I don't see as how you'll find another one like him out here."

"Who says I am even looking for a man?"

"My lady, you are young and beautiful and dare I say it, you're wealthy. But even worse, you're a land owner in your own right, with your claim paid for. There's trouble brewing if you don't find a man. Even out here in the middle of nowhere, with no one in sight and no one in the way, believe you me... men will find you, and they may not be the kind of honorable men Mr. MacAteer seems to be." Her commanding tone softened to one of loving respect for her mistress. "And besides, you'll want to be married someday and have a family of your own, so what's not to like about a man who has gone to all the trouble to bring you here? Mr.

MacAteer certainly seemed disappointed enough that you hadn't come to be his wife."

Moira had no reply. This wasn't a conversation she'd meant to have with anyone, least of all her serving girl, because it would have meant she had to acknowledge her own feelings on the matter. It was far safer to tell herself Pryor was off-limits, that he was only a fellow settler, someone who could help her on her way and nothing more. She had no time nor inclination for a complication such as her feelings for Pryor, no matter how much they continued to peck at her mind.

"Admit it, my lady," Gretchen prodded kindly, giving Moira an encouraging look. "You care for the man. And you know he cares for you."

She wanted to stand her ground, but instead, found herself nodding without even realizing it. "He's a kind, honest, and hard-working man if ever there was one. But I cannot waste my time on a schoolgirl's idea of love and romance. I am here to establish the Brennan claim, and nothing more."

"Are you still holding onto the hope that Ronan will come for you?"

"No, that's not it," Moira admitted, dropping her gaze to her hands. Gretchen wasn't convinced, but didn't press her point; she didn't need to, as her mistress read her thoughts perfectly. "It's just that I had that dream for so long that I'm not ready to let go of it. In my mind, it would all turn out fine, and my family would be pleased to have a greater estate, and my husband, who my father had chosen with my blessing, would oversee the American holdings. It was all going to be perfect, and now it shall never be."

"Oh, my lady, you do not know what will come to pass. And if this dream never happens, then you'll seize upon a new dream, one that lifts your spirits in the same way this one did. But there's no reason that the dream of working your land with your husband has to be dashed. Don't decide it now, ma'am, but promise your heart that you won't shut love out."

That had been the night before, but Gretchen's words had prevented Moira from having a sound night's sleep. As a result, she'd yawned her way through breakfast and now practically nodded off sitting upright in the wagon, a strong urge to nap suddenly brought on by the swaying of the cart as the horses moved. The occasional rock or ridge in the path jolted her every time, her neck nearly snapping in two whenever the wagon moved too sharply.

All of a sudden, there was no way Moira could have slept, not even with a draught and a week without sleep, for Pryor guided the horses around a bend and the valley below came into view. The creek that wound through Pryor's property to carry water from the river some miles away worked its way through the land here, providing a bubbling backdrop to the vista.

"This is mine?" she whispered, trembling so visibly that Gretchen reached a hand out to comfort her, to convince her it was real.

"Yup, this is your land," Pryor agreed, watching her face as the realization set in. The look of rapturous joy was one he knew well, because he remembered the same feeling etched on his expression when he first saw his homestead. "Are you going to get out and visit, or was just this one look enough for ya?"

Moira grinned and jumped down from the wagon without waiting for Gretchen or Pryor to help her. She ran forward, her simple skirt flying out behind her as she moved, anxious to feel the land beneath her own feet. She stopped and threw herself down, ripping her boots and stockings off without bothering with the buttons. She screamed with laughter when she finally felt the grass tickling her bare toes, while Pryor and Gretchen looked on in shock and amusement.

"My lady?" her maid asked, climbing down from the wagon and walking over to her hesitantly. "Are you feeling all right?"

"Oh, Gretchen, my dear! I'm far better than all right! I'm home! Look out upon this place, this is our home!" She let out a loud yell as she jumped up and continued to run, weaving a path through the land that carried her over and around the contours of the land. She'd run all the way to the creek before Pryor could tie off his horses on their picket line and let them eat the grass. When he flopped down in the shade of the wagon and rested with his arms behind his head, Gretchen stared between the two of them, wondering what to do.

"Should we go after her?" she finally asked, keeping a respectable distance from the man who was reclining on the ground very close to her feet. Pryor didn't open his eyes to answer.

"Naw. She knows where the wagon is. It's best to let her enjoy this moment; she'll come back when she's had her fill of running and yelling and exploring."

"You describe her as though she was a hunting dog, Mr. MacAteer!" Gretchen chastised with a light laugh.

"She might as well be at this moment, but don't you dare tell her I said that!" He laughed softly, a sound that grew suspiciously into a snore. Gretchen walked away apiece to give him his privacy during a much needed rest, and to keep a closer eye on her mistress. What she couldn't see was Pryor waiting until Gretchen had moved down the hill before propping himself up on one bent elbow, watching happily and protectively as Moira reveled in her new find.

After an hour of exploring, Moira had still only seen the first few acres. She plotted in her mind where the cabin would go, where a modest barn could be built, where she could position some animals to graze, where she could plant a garden. It was more than a little overwhelming to envision it all, especially with Gretchen's words from the night before still moving around in her thoughts.

Was there any truth to what the maid had said? Did she really want to linger out in her home, beautiful though it may be, alone as a spinster woman? Or could she put aside her prejudice long enough to know that not every man and every marriage had to be a prison?

Moira turned to look back toward the wagon and was shocked at how far away it seemed. The tiny speck at the top of the hill made her feel small against the landscape somehow, and the sight of her maid walking closer was a welcome relief. Perhaps Gretchen had been right, and she wasn't looking to throw caution to the wind and live in the frontier.

"Gretchen!" Moira called, waving her arms to bring the girl closer. "Come and have a look!" When the maid finally came to the spot where Moira stood, she was somewhat out of breath, but smiling all the same.

"It is a beautiful property, my lady," Gretchen said, shielding her eyes from the sun with her hand as she looked in every direction. "But it's so…"

"What? What's the matter?" Moira demanded, turning and watching her maid's expression.

"It's just so far… from everything. What will we do if we need something, or if there's danger?"

"We'll have to learn to fend for ourselves, that's what

we'll do!" Moira replied, standing up taller and throwing her shoulders back, puffing out her chest with an air of confidence. Gretchen looked much less certain, but Moira noticed she didn't offer any argument. "Is it really that alarming to you to be so isolated?"

Gretchen weighed her answer carefully. The last thing she wanted to do was to sink Moira's spirits, not after she'd come so far. She merely shrugged her shoulders instead of having to answer directly, and Moira threw her arm around the girl's shoulders.

"We will be fine, you'll see! This is where our new adventure begins, the place we've worked so hard to come to! Come, let us tell Pryor we want his thoughts on where to put up a house and a barn, and we'll want to know what supplies he recommends."

They trudged back up the slope of the land, taking their time as they inspected the hillside. The plans and possibilities swirled in Moira's mind all the way back to where Pryor waited for them.

CHAPTER FIFTEEN

Several hours later, they were back in New Hope for the first time since Moira and Gretchen had arrived, and neither could believe that it had only been a few days ago that they'd stepped off the train and into the sullen emptiness. Today, though, was an altogether different day, as wagons rolled through the one wide street and settlers walked among the handful of buildings. At least a third of the town's claimed population had business to attend to, and it was no small relief to Gretchen to see so many other human faces after going days without anyone but her two companions for company.

"Where have all these people come from?" Moira asked in a hushed voice, suddenly suspicious of so many strange people. "Surely they cannot all live close to New Hope?"

"That they do," Pryor said with a nod. "A good number more. But you're just scratching the surface of how big this whole region is. When you think that most of these people each have a claim the size of yours, and the size of mine, it really makes you think just how huge the frontier is. It's certainly something to think about."

Moira and Gretchen watched from the wagon as it rolled through the thoroughfare, looking from person to person and trying not to stare.

"Gretchen, what do you notice about these people?" Moira asked in a whisper, leaning close so no one would see them talking together.

"I can naw say, miss. They seem... I dunno, I haven't put my finger on it just yet." Gretchen turned around to watch a cluster of men emerge from one of the businesses, and followed them with her eyes as they entered an adjacent store to finish gathering the things they needed. "They don't look... happy?"

"That's it," Moira agreed with a curt nod of her head. "They all look weary and downtrodden! Is this what the life of a homesteader looks like? Where is the pleasure of owning your own property and increasing your farm? That feeling I myself had but a few hours ago?"

"I could naw say, my lady. Perhaps it's from knowing that their farms aren't in the clear yet?"

"I hope you're right. Because if not, I'm in way over my head! I don't want to look like these people! They look bone tired and sad, even the women."

"Especially the women, you mean," Gretchen said with a wry look, nodding almost imperceptibly at a family of a husband and a wife and eight children climbing down from a wagon. Moira's eyes went wide.

"And here Ronan was angry that that old goat Macomby lets his wives die in their child beds for want of a doctor. Where on earth would a doctor even come from out here, do you wonder?" Gretchen turned a deep shade of pink at what her lady was referring to, but just shook her head in agreement.

"But Mr. MacAteer doesn't look this way. How is it that he's so much livelier than some of this bunch? Some of these people are more skeleton than man, with naught any meat on their bones."

"I dare not ask him for fear he'd tell me I could expect to be unhappy like this lot," Moira answered. "Perhaps it's the success of his harvest? Maybe all of these people drew claims with poor soil, like that Mr. Russell?"

"That's quite ominous, my lady."

"How do you mean?"

"Don't you think there'd be fighting over the land? Mr. MacAteer already said there was no lawman in New Hope, perhaps 'twas because he had too much work to do keeping the homesteaders in line!"

They were prevented from any more speculation when Pryor pulled back on the reins, bringing the horses' slow walk to a stop in front of the largest of the wooden buildings in the town, if town was even the right word. He climbed down and secured their line to a horizontal post that ran in front of the store, then turned and offered his hand to Gretchen and then to Moira. He gestured for them to follow him as he ducked his head and entered the low door of the building, designed intentionally small to let in light but keep out the snow and winds of the cold Montana winters.

They stepped down into the store, a surprise considering its low height. Once they reached the dirt floor, they could see that the walls actually extended well above their heads and that dry goods and other implements lined every inch of space, even reaching into and across the rafters. The structure put the windows high up on the walls so that light drifted down to the ground below, illuminating the shelves and their wares.

"Hallo, Mac!" an older gentleman called out in an accent that was strange to the women's ears. They turned to find a man with the whitest hair they'd ever seen climbing down from a ladder secured to the wall on rails. He dusted his hands off on his thick apron and shook hands with Pryor before turning his attention to the ladies. "Ah, yes! I forgot all about how we'd mailed off that letter for a bride! Is this the wife, then?"

Pryor bristled at the reminder, but shrugged it off and turned to Moira, who stood ramrod straight and blushed. He shook his head sadly.

"Alas, no!" he said dramatically. "She's fresh off the boat from Ireland, and that temper would take years off my life, I tell ya. I'd be a dead man before this time next year if I crossed her! I'm thinking about sending her back and getting a nice Scandinavian girl, someone like your wife!"

The girls exchanged a horrified look at the brutish but joking exchange, but smiled when Pryor turned his attention back to them. "Miss Brennan, Miss… Gretchen," he began, frowning when he realized he didn't know the maid's full name. "This is Mr. Jorgenson, who owns the mercantile. This will be where you come for any supplies you need." He turned back to the shopkeeper. "Miss Brennan has just come out here, and has a claim about twenty miles past my place."

"Is that right?" the old man asked, a look mixed with disbelief and pride on his face. "You're going to make it out here? The two of you?"

"Yes, sir, we are," Moira began, but Pryor cut her off before she could divulge too much more about herself.

"And that's why the first thing on the lady's list is a good sturdy gun. Let me know if you'll have to order one, and I can loan her something lightweight until it comes by train."

"No, no, we have quite a few right now, let me go see what I can find in the back. Something effective, but that won't send her sprawling on her backside!" The old man tottered off to one of the storerooms in the back of the building, leaving Moira to cock an eyebrow at Pryor.

"Irish temper? *Miss* Brennan? My... *backside*?!" she hissed, staring up at him with an angry fire in her eyes. "I've never been so insulted by a man who was allowed to remain standing after speaking like that!"

"What do you mean?" Pryor asked, blinking in surprise.

"My name is Lady Moira Brennan, first of all, a fact that I would happily overlook if you hadn't introduced me as the woman you were sending back because I was a cranky, ill-tempered husband murdering wench!"

"Hey! Keep your voice down! You don't to go throwing around that 'Lady Brennan' stuff out here!"

"And why is that? 'Tis my name, is it not?" She struggled to lower her voice, chagrined to realize that her "Irish temper" was in full force and made for a well-deserved generalization.

"It might have been back where you came from, but I've already told you, that's not the way of things here. Half these men are here because their governments in their own countries weren't the nicest of people. You go letting everyone know you're royalty, and you'll find you have a lot of trouble conducting business and making acquaintances. Even worse, any of these fine folks could get it in their heads that you have money, and trust me, that's a dangerous rumor to let out."

Moira opened her mouth to retort but quickly clamped it shut. She looked around furtively, seeing the same bedraggled homesteaders as before, but now seeing them in a menacing light. Beside her, Gretchen turned sickly looking and trembled slightly before her mistress linked her arm through her own protectively.

Moira closed her eyes for only a moment, then spoke. "I'm very sorry, Pryor, I had no idea you were acting to protect us. I apologize sincerely."

"Don't worry yourself about it, Moira," he said with a mischievous look. "I know you can't help it, what with that Irish temper." He chuckled and walked away to look at some store goods before she could say anything else.

CHAPTER SIXTEEN

The wagon finally rolled up to Pryor's cabin sometime close to midnight. It had been a long, adventurous day filled with wonder, but filled with confusion as well. Moira still didn't know what to make of her experience in New Hope, choosing to focus most of her thoughts on her land instead. Her elation had been diminished a little, not just by the town and her understanding of her precarious position, but in her land, too.

Seeing the wares in Jorgenson's store gave Moira a long overdue dose of reality. She had a cabin to build, a fence to erect around her property, livestock to acquire and breed—after building a barn, of course—and crops to plant. At that very moment, Moira had not so much as a carrot to put in a root cellar against the following winter, nor the root cellar to put it in. She would have to make it through the coming harsh months before she could do any of those things, and would have to live on her own funds until such time as she could begin investing in her property.

It was only then that she realized she'd acted out of desperation rather than foresight. A smarter individual would have held off until the spring, waiting for the worst of the weather to pass before trying to build a home site. But time wasn't a luxury she'd had, and in her hurry to take herself far away from Brennan, from Macomby's madness and from Ronan's demise, she hadn't thought any farther ahead than the following month.

Now, the reality of her situation was upon her, worming its way into her conscience for the hundredth time and making her feel doubt and fear. Was this the same feeling that made all those other girls accept the advertisements and marry a stranger on the frontier? A feeling of loneliness coupled with knowing they had no way to survive on their own?

No. Moira vowed to herself right then that she would never marry because she simply needed to be taken care of. If she ever chose to marry, and the chances of the situation ever presenting itself were not high, it would be because she felt in her heart that it was what she wanted, not something that she needed to do to make sure there was food in her belly and a warm fire beside her bed.

But what would she do to survive the winter, and to ensure that Gretchen was well cared for as well?

"Hey, you back there, we're home," Pryor called back quietly, before realizing the implication of what he'd said. This wasn't their home, and thanks to his supposed bride and her newfound sense of independence, it never would be a home. He'd been so happy today that he'd forgotten for a moment that he was still going to end up alone in the vast frontier.

Both Moira and Gretchen had fallen asleep, curled up side by side. It had been a day filled with adventure and new experiences for both of them, so it came as little surprise that they would be fast asleep, especially given the late hour.

He hesitated to rouse them but certainly didn't want them to wake up feeling out of sorts.

Pryor opened the barn doors wide but unhitched the team out of doors, ignoring the confused stomping of their hooves as he pulled them out of their traces. He tended to them first, feeding and watering and brushing them down before putting them in their stalls and tossing a forkful of hay over the low stall doors. Then he turned his attention to the wagon, checking to make sure the passengers were still sound asleep before pushing against it with all his might, rolling it laboriously through the open doors until it was secured under the roof. He lit a fresh wick on the lantern and hung it from its post nail in the barn, then closed the door and locked it, blocking the light of the full moon that had guided his work. Finally, he covered the two ladies with a blanket from the wagon seat, tucking it around them carefully before settling himself down on his usual bed of hay in one of the empty stalls.

Pryor lay awake for far too long, staring at the roof overhead and catching the few slivers of moonlight that showed him where he needed to patch his roof the next time he had reason to work with tar pitch. His short time in the territory had taught him that small problems were best handled while they were still little. If he waited until a small issue became large, he ran the risk of ruin.

I could say the same about Moira, he thought suddenly, surprising himself at bringing up her name. *She's not a problem*, he argued in his head, but even he knew that wasn't true. She was most definitely a problem, a small problem to be sure, but one that was certain to turn into a big problem if he didn't do something about it soon.

The sound of the animals getting their early breakfast woke Moira the next morning. She sat upright in the wagon, hay sticking out of her hair, and looked around in bewilderment. The last thing she remembered was watching the stars dot the sky over the wagon as it moved along, but suddenly, she found herself in the barn, surrounded by the noise of work already being done. Beside her, an empty dent in the hay told her that Gretchen had been nearby, but was already awake and most likely putting together a meal for them in the house.

She climbed down from the wagon and turned to join her maid, but ran straight into Pryor's solid chest instead. The fright of it caused her to cry out in disbelief, but she was kept from falling backwards by two warm, firm hands that captured her elbows and held her close. Moira found herself looking almost straight up in order to see Pryor's face above hers. She gasped quietly, but was left bereft when his hands immediately released her. She put out a hand to steady herself against the wagon, waiting for the right words to come to her.

"Thank you for saving me from falling," she finally managed when she was able to command her voice to stop betraying her. "And for making us a warm, safe bed for the night. I hope we didn't disturb your animals by encroaching on their homes."

Pryor wasn't to be distracted so easily by talk of manners. He'd not yet let himself imagine holding Moira in his arms, and that brief contact had been enough to render him speechless, not that he had been a man of many words before meeting her. Lately he found himself talking to her throughout the day, explaining things about homesteading that were either vital or trivial, but enjoying the conversation with her all the same. Now, though, he had nothing to say, not even an utterance to cover his embarrassment at having grabbed hold of her.

Moira, though, was stung by a flood of embarrassment of her own. The man had only prevented her from toppling over, but she praised him as though he'd plucked her out of a raging river. She'd only spoken up to have something to say, and instead, she'd gone and made him so uncomfortable, he wouldn't even answer. She ducked her head and turned to go in the house, muttering about helping Gretchen with their meal, when Pryor put out one and hand and stopped her, clinging gently to her elbow to keep her from leaving.

"Moira, wait." She stopped and held her breath, unable to keep from looking down at his hand to see if it was actually leaving a mark where the heat of his skin pierced through her cotton shirt. He misinterpreted her look, and immediately pulled his hand back. It was enough to keep him from speaking any further. Instead of begging her to sit, to listen to him plead for their contract, however false or accidental it may have been, he nodded solemnly and turned back to pitching hay to his horses.

Moira took a tentative step toward the door, not wanting to leave with the air so tense between them. Whatever it was that he'd been about to say couldn't have just disappeared altogether. If she waited long enough, maybe he'd find the nerve to speak again.

Suddenly, Pryor brightened as a new idea came to him. He'd wracked his brain all during the night to come up with a reason for Moira to stay, and not just stay in the territory, but to stay close by him. Whether it was fear of her leaving, or the tiny stab at his heart that he felt each time she walked away from him, as though it could be the last time she walked away from him, a new plan formed in his mind, one that could hopefully keep Moira close.

CHAPTER SEVENTEEN

"**A**re you sure you won't tell me where we're going? Not even a small hint?" Moira asked again, ignoring the rebellious look in Pryor's eye, the look that told her he wasn't going to divulge anything before it was time.

They'd left Gretchen at the cabin, much to the girl's horror given what would ordinarily be scandalous behavior, and ridden out on the horses to the north of Pryor's claim, heading back in the direction of New Hope, despite the man's promise that they wouldn't be going nearly that far. They hadn't even saddled the horses, so Moira knew the distance couldn't be all that great.

"No, ma'am. If I tell you now, you won't have any reason to listen politely while I tell it to the other fella."

"What other 'fella'?" Moira demanded.

"I can't tell you that either. If I tell you who the other fella is, you'll know where we're going!" He winked at her, a tiny flicker of mannerism that had the effect of nearly stopping her heart. She blinked and cleared her mind of any thoughts about Pryor's good looks, and forced herself to think instead about finding her bearings in the wide open plain.

"Okay, you twisted my arm," Pryor began, but a bewildered look on Moira's face made him laugh. "Sorry, I mean, you convinced me. That's frontier talk for 'you convinced me' if it ever comes up again."

"I see. And what did I convince you of, exactly?"

"I'll give you a little hint about where we're going."

"Oh, good! I was beginning to think we were riding these poor animals back to New Hope, after dragging them all over the territory yesterday."

"No, but it's not like these two couldn't handle the work! They're some of the finest in this part of the country. And that's partly what I wanted to talk to you about, and why we're going visiting today."

"Visiting? Are we going to see your friend, Mr. Russell?"

"Yes, but don't let him hear you calling him that! Lady or not, he doesn't take kindly to fancy talk," Pryor teased, but he quickly turned serious again. "He's actually part of why I wanted to go ride with you this morning, away from... just to go with you and talk to you."

Moira could sense from his tone and cryptic words that this was to be no ordinary pleasant visit. There was a sense about him that was both ominous and exciting, while still keeping her wholly unaware of what he could possibly be thinking. She knew just enough about men, and people in general, to know what his unfinished sentence would have said, though, if he'd been able to bring himself to finish it.

...away from Gretchen.

So Pryor wanted to speak to her alone, did he? The thought was both unnerving and thrilling. It went against her entire upbringing and social class to even be riding with him without a chaperone, let alone the fact that they were paying a call to another man, a man who owned property, without having first sent a message ahead through a servant.

It was amazing to discover that the things that once defined her, that she once held dear as the characteristics that distinguished a well-bred lady from a servant in the household, were no longer important. It hardly seemed possible that only a little more than two months ago, she'd been dining in her brother's hall each evening, finely dressed and exquisitely fed. Only six months ago, she had overseen the preparations for her father's birthday celebration, a week-long affair with three separate but equally extravagant parties for different varieties of guests.

Now, she had nothing of the sort, yet she was oddly at peace with her choice. There would be no gala occasions or even simple family holidays anymore. Although it pained her to think of missing her brother and any family he grew for himself, the opulence she was accustomed to at holidays wasn't all that important. Fulfilling her obligation to her claim and surviving were all that mattered.

"We're here, princess," Pryor announced, interrupting Moira's thoughts.

"Oh, please don't call me that, I'm hardly a princess," she answered, but stopped when she realized he was only being playful. She smirked at him before turning her attention to the property.

Her heart felt like it had dropped into her stomach at the same time that her breakfast threatened to come up. This property was nothing like Pryor's neat, efficient farm. Instead, it appeared as though there had been an explosion of some kind, one that had scattered lumber and metal and farm implements all around the once-grassy slope in piles of abandoned debris. She recovered quickly and managed to not pass judgment, at least not in a way anyone could see.

"Yeah, I kind of thought you'd feel that way," Pryor said as if reading her thoughts. She smiled politely in order to keep anyone else from figuring out how she felt about the sight before her.

"What happened?" she asked quietly.

"Like I said, Nathanial struggled to get his feet under him, then finally had to just walk away from it and try to build up enough capital to start fresh."

"But that doesn't explain the hole through the roof!"

"No, that's just a matter of him not having the time or skills to get it finished. Now, I know what you're thinking, and you're wrong. He's not lazy, not in the least, but this kind of task is too great for some people to take on."

"I wasn't thinking that he's lazy! And what are you trying to imply? Did you bring me here to frighten me out of settling my claim?"

"What?" Pryor demanded, obviously confused by her accusation.

"Let me rephrase my question so that you better understand my meaning then," she said in a hissed whisper. "Did you bring me all this way to Mr. Russell's land just to demonstrate that a fully grown and otherwise capable man wasn't able to even build himself a shelter, so I shouldn't expect to be able to either?"

"I wouldn't do that! If you'll just wait, you'll understand why I brought you here. Now, come on, he's already seen us through the window." Pryor climbed down from his horse and tied it off on the fence rail, or what was left of it, before reaching up a hand to help Moira down.

She was not to be won over so easily, not when her pride and this man's cunning were at stake. She slid down from the horse on her own before looking triumphantly up at

Pryor. She held out her arm for him to lead the way, given that this was his acquaintance.

"Hallow, Russell!" Pryor called out, waving an open hand at the face that appeared again in the window. Nathaniel waved and smiled, beckoning them inside excitedly. He opened the door and called out to Pryor, then grabbed his hand and shook it hard. "You're looking well for a railroad man!"

"Aye, and I'm feeling well, too! Come in, come in!" He turned and led the way into the dark cabin, lit only by the sunlight that came through the small square windows, gaping holes that still didn't have glass, dotting the thick, rough walls.

Nathaniel kicked aside some more debris that had been piled up inside the house, shoving an unfolded stack of linens to the floor then kicking them into a corner to make room for his guests to sit. He brushed crumbs from the table and swept them into his hand, tossing them out one of the windows without looking over his shoulder to see where they landed.

"So is this your new wife you told me about?" Nathaniel asked, without waiting for proper introductions. Moira tried once again to keep a pleasant look on her face, but noticed this time, it wasn't quite as funny to Pryor. Perhaps he, too, was growing weary of the question, and even more weary of wondering why it wasn't real.

"No, this is Miss Brennan, another landowner. I heard you met her maid at the creek the other day, the one doing the washing?"

"Oh, of course! I remember that one, the pretty one! She didn't talk much, she seemed kinda shy. But she sure had a pretty smile!" Nathaniel had a dreamy look on his face for a moment, but shook it off as he turned back to the two visitors. "So, you two came out riding today and stopped by? That girl must have given you my message!"

Moira noticed that everything seemed to fill Nathaniel with excitement and wonder, as every remark he made was punctuated with extra emphasis. He struck her as a man who was just happy to be anywhere, let alone in the wide open of the frontier. It seemed no wonder, then, given that he'd been working on blasting the mountains through with tunnels. The days and weeks spent in the dark of the mountain passes must have been like being buried alive; it was no wonder that he could take such joy from a simple visit in an even simpler home.

The three of them chatted pleasantly, but when Pryor noticed Moira begin to look wilted, he suggested they all head back outside to the shade of the small porch.

"I don't know if this is the right time to speak up or not..." Pryor begin, dropping his gaze to his lap as he waited for the right words. "But I have a proposal to make for the two of you. It's going to seem a little strange coming from me, and I hope you'll hear me out and think it over before you answer."

Moira saw spots before her eyes and realized she was holding her breath. She felt faint, and not just from the dusty air inside the house. She couldn't believe what she was hearing. Could it be that Pryor was really suggesting what she thought he was? Now that there was no contract between them, was he passing her off to Nathaniel? Images of a lifetime serving a madman in a rundown shack flooded her brain, nearly blocking out all other sensation and preventing her from hearing his next words.

"I propose... that you, Moira, take Nathaniel's claim, and sell your claim to him."

For his part, Nathaniel looked confused, but not more

than Moira. The relief of not being offered to yet a third stranger in marriage made her almost giddy, but Pryor's words were equally strange. Give Nathaniel her claim? And pay even more to buy another man's property?

"I'm not sure I understand," Nathaniel said, speaking up before Moira had a chance to. At least she wasn't the only one to think the whole scenario odd.

"Here's the way I see it," Pryor continued. "Nathaniel, we all know nothing will grow on your land. You came out to be a farmer and to grow wheat, but it won't happen. You could spend the next twenty years harvesting nothing but the rocks on your place, and you still wouldn't be able to plant out here. But Moira... pardon me, I mean, Miss Brennan... has no plans to farm. She'll definitely keep a garden, and she'll need to plant a variety of hay if she keeps any livestock, but other than that, her land is in the clear. She doesn't have to grow so much as a blade of grass if she don't want to!

"And as for you, Moira, have you given any thought to how you're going to live? To building a house, and a barn? You have a wonderful plot, but not so much as a canvas and a stick to keep the rain off. So here's what I wanted to say. Moira signs her claim over to Nathaniel, Nathaniel signs his claim over to Moira. Nathaniel keeps any farming tools he's bought, but in exchange for the house and the barn he's already begun and all the lumber and nails needed to finish it, Moira pays the final portion on this claim. That sets Nathaniel up to not owe on his claim, freeing up his earnings from the railroad to build himself a new house and work on his fence. Moira would simply need to improve this house, and finish the fence Nathaniel has already started."

Pryor sat back in his chair looking very much like King Solomon, his wisdom spreading over any situation.

Nathaniel and Moira both sat pondering the situation he'd presented, weighing its consequences against what each stood to gain.

It didn't escape Moira's notice that Pryor's plan kept her within close distance of his property, rather than the hours-long ride to her own place. She fought back a smile, but her heart warmed at this new understanding of the man she was still getting to know.

CHAPTER EIGHTEEN

Moira and Nathaniel shook on the deal after much deliberation. Pryor looked on as a witness to the deal, and Moira wrote up the various bills of sale that gave Nathaniel her claim outright, while she agreed to provide the rest of Nathaniel's claim on her new property. A small part of her brain wondered if this was like her uncle's scheme to get her brother out of the way to inherit Brennan Castle and all that went with it, but she decided that Pryor's explanation made perfect sense. She didn't come to America to pick up a plow, she'd come to live in the solitude that wide open spaces could provide. What need did she have of a valley of fertile soil, when she didn't intend to work the land?

Nathaniel, on the other hand, had worked himself to the bone to try to farm his claim, and only ended up turning to hard labor to pay his bills. It only made sense that he should have the chance to succeed, the same chance everyone who'd come West was looking for.

Nathaniel invited them to stay for supper, but Moira

wouldn't think of taking his hospitality when he was so newly returned to his home. That, and she wasn't sure she trusted the conditions enough to eat anything in the house without witnessing a thorough scrubbing for herself.

"I'm sorry I didn't tell you about my plan sooner," Pryor said, breaking the comfortable silence between them as they rode back to his cabin. "I didn't want to worry you by having you think you were being swindled, so I wanted you to hear it for the first time when Nathaniel did."

"No, it's quite all right. I admit, it was a bit of a surprise, of course, but it is a sound plan. It appears to benefit both Mr. Russell and myself equally. I am a bit concerned, though, about the state of his home. It's not quite what I imagined living in when I spent all those weeks in a cramped ship's cabin, to be followed by more weeks of sitting upright on a train!" Moira was teasing, but there was still a ring of truth. In this proposal, she ended up with the very house that she couldn't envision eating a meal in, let alone living in.

"There's nothing to worry about there, I'll be happy to help finish the house. Nathaniel's one of the best and has a heart of gold, I just don't think he was prepared for homesteading. He's a city dweller, if I remember his story correctly, and didn't know much about building a shelter. That's why I said the lumber had to be included. His barn is pretty sound, though. I should know, I helped him build it!"

Moira laughed, uncertain of the connection between Pryor's own pristine farm and the piles of refuse that made up Nathaniel's place. It hardly seemed possible that he'd had a hand in anything that even touched that farm... her farm, she realized with a surprising sense of satisfaction.

"Tell me honestly, Pryor, was it any coincidence that you requested this move?"

"What do you mean?" he asked, but in his heart he knew what she was getting at. Moira paused before answering, but finally decided to simply say it.

"I mean, does your plan have to do with keeping me closer to your farm?"

"Why, Moira. I'm surprised at you. Do you think I would really go to that trouble and have you move just so you could be closer in case of problems, or if you had need of something, or just so I could see you whenever I wanted?" His tone was light and playful, but she could sense a different truth to his words. The realization made her blush. They had not even broached the subject of their alleged contract since their first unpleasant talk, and they hadn't truly reached a resolution. She did not feel right assuming there was anything more than supportive camaraderie between them, but she couldn't put aside the feeling that there was more to this.

"That isn't an answer, and you know it," she replied confidently.

"Maybe I did want you to be closer. Does that upset you?"

"No," she answered, realizing that it was not at all a lie. "Is that why you did it?"

"Well, it really does make perfect sense for the two of you to move. If you happen to be my neighbor, then that's just a good thing."

Moira was surprised at how crestfallen she was by his answer. It was not a resounding declaration of anything more than convenience, let alone affection. Pryor noticed that she had not answered, and stole a quick glance at her. The look of hurt he saw unnerved him, and gave him something close to hope.

"Of course, there's always that contract..." he said, but

left the rest of his sentence hanging in the space between them. Moira didn't look up right away, giving herself time to make sure she'd heard him correctly.

"Yes, I suppose there is," she answered, still looking down.

"And if we saw it through, then our properties would be joined, too."

At that, Moira did turn up and look at Pryor sharply, a fresh anger burning behind her eyes. "So that's what this was all about! You led me astray and betrayed your own friend to get a bigger farm? First, I'm just a stranger you brought out here to work and give you children, and then, I'm just a piece of property? No, thank you!"

She spurred her horse forward, ignoring Pryor's cries behind her as he shouted her name over and over. She couldn't hear it over the sound of the wind rushing past her ears, a blessed sound that she hadn't heard in too long, not since taking her own beloved horse for their last ride. The wind was even more welcomed as it pushed away the sound of Pryor's voice, and almost pushed away the memory of his words.

Even as an accomplished horsewoman, Moira had trouble controlling the horse. As a draft animal, it never had the opportunity to run in a wide-open, unfettered way, so when Moira gave the command the animal charged forward, free from the weight of a wagon or a plot, eager to release the pent up energy in its capable muscles. It startled her how fast the horse took off, and without a saddle or normal bridle and reins, she had trouble staying upright. She held fast with her legs though, determined to put Pryor and his conniving attempts at gaining more land through trickery and flattery behind her.

With one final burst of speed, Moira and the horse

surged forward, heading for the creek and intent on putting distance between the cabin and herself. She couldn't hear Pryor anymore and knew he'd finally given up and turned toward his cabin. She could only hope that he'd realized how wrong he was about the potential for his arrangement. She'd never marry him, not even if he begged her. Not even if he signed over his own land... why should she be the one to bring property to a marriage and then turn it over to her husband? It was Brennan and Macomby all over again.

The sound of Moira's own scream startled her, ripping her from her miserable thoughts. The horse stalled beneath her, unsure of itself as it reached the water's edge. Rather than sail over the gently rushing water, the horse stopped, sending Moira careening over its shoulder and landing with a sharp crack in the water, her head opened by the edge of a rock. The water was freezing cold and almost enough to snap her out of the darkness of pain that had wrapped around her, but the blackness quickly took over.

When she opened her eyes some time later, a heavy cloth pressed over her forehead prevented her from seeing. Moira couldn't tell where she was, other than from the comforting and already familiar smell of fresh soap coming from the pillow cover. She knew she was in Pryor's cabin, but couldn't remember what had happened or how she'd gotten there. She moved to take Gretchen's hand off her eyes, and was surprised to feel a rough, work worn hand there instead.

"Oh, no, you don't, don't try to move just yet. You've broken something, to be sure," Pryor said gently. He peeled back the cloth to let a little bit of lamp light shine on her face, but even that made her squint her eyes against the harsh glare. A pounding pain in her head immediately made her want to throw up, and she pressed her free hand to her stomach to calm the feeling. Her other hand was bound against her side with strips of cloth, which only dulled the stabbing pain she now felt in her shoulder.

"What happened?" she tried to ask, but her voice was raspy from thirst.

"You ran away from me, that's what happened," he chided, but there was kindness in his voice, most likely brought on from the relief of hearing Moira speak and seeing her open her eyes. "Your horse threw you at the water's edge, and you hit your head. It seems you've broken your collar bone, too. But, look, now you have a scar like mine!"

He pushed back the hair over his forehead to show the stitches that still held him together, then laughed. "But don't worry, yours didn't require any needlework, thank goodness. When I carried you inside, I'm sorry to say your maid fainted dead away at the sight of your blood. She'd have been useless if you'd needed stitching, and I think you know how my sewing skills compare to yours. Without my clumsy fingers tying you in knots, I dare say your scar is going to be a lot fairer than mine."

"Tis some small comfort to know I wasn't disfigured by my own stupidity," she replied, closing her eyes again and adjusting to the feelings of pain and sickness. She tried to sit up suddenly with a gasp, but Pryor held her good shoulder fast. "Wait, you said Gretchen fainted? Where is she, is she all right?"

"She's fine. She recovered quickly, and she even apologized for being helpless when you needed her. We fixed her a bed of blankets in the front room so she wouldn't shake you during the night." Pryor spoke again, softly, not wanting to upset or hurt her. "Why did you run away?"

"I should think it would be obvious, at least from a lady who's accustomed to having men decide what will happen to her."

"Do you mean your land?"

"Of course."

"I don't want your land, Moira. I only said that because I wanted you to know that you would have my land if we were married. Remember, you agreed to take a plot that won't grow anything, and I wanted you to know that anything I harvest becomes yours, too, if we married, that is. I would never take something from you."

Moira was quiet as tears pricked at her eyes. "You already have, Pryor. You took my heart, and I certainly did not intend for you to have it."

"Then I shall have to return it to you, just to keep you happy." Moira opened her eyes a crack and looked at him, and saw that he was deadly serious. "Yes, if that's what it takes to keep you happy, I will leave you alone."

"And if I don't want to be alone?"

"Then that will have to be for you to decide. But be quick. I've been alone, for a long time even, and after a while, you learn how to get by. You won't ever be happy and you won't ever thrive, but you'll learn how to manage it all in solitude." Pryor smiled thinly, explaining more in those few words than a lifetime of her previous understanding about people and want had ever done.

They stayed in the relative darkness of the cabin's room, the lamp and a lingering moonlight providing more than enough light to cover the shy glances on their faces.

"I don't want to be alone, Pryor. But more than that, I don't want to be without you. I had more than enough chances to marry if that's all I wanted, but it wasn't enough for me. I would rather be alone like you say than be bound to the wrong man. And somehow, I just know you're the right man."

"Do you really mean that? You would go through with the contract?"

"No, not for a minute." Pryor looked crestfallen before Moira continued, "I would never marry you because you paid a broker's fee and sent me a piece of paper. But I will marry you because you are kind, and honorable, and giving to others. You think of everyone else before yourself, and yet, you've still made yourself the richest man in the territory by being content with what you have. That is why I will marry you, not because of an agreement I don't even remember entering into."

Pryor smiled broadly before surpassing his grin. "Excuse me, I have to see to something."

He got abruptly and left the room, and only seconds later, Moira heard the front door of the cabin open and close. Thundering footsteps on the porch told her that Pryor had quite literally just run away. She knit her brow in confusion but quickly recoiled from the pain where a thin scab had already formed. She pressed her hand to the wound to make sure it hadn't opened, but shuddered when an unholy howl pierced the night outside her window. Her fear quickly turned to quiet laughter when she realized the sound was coming from Pryor, whose long note of joy turned into shouts of happiness.

CHAPTER NINETEEN

"**A**re you sure? It doesn't have to be today, not with your arm still hurt," Pryor reminded Moira for the hundredth time. She smiled and adjusted her hat.

"My arm is fine. It's just a little sore, that's all. Besides, aren't you quite ready to stop sleeping in the barn? It's been over a month; you must be getting tired of telling your horses goodnight!"

Pryor smiled at his soon-to-be bride. The past month had been a surreal time of preparation and activity for both of them. The land exchange between Moira and Nathaniel had been finalized, with the rest of the claim paid for outright. Pryor had taken the time to add a room onto their house for Gretchen, one that extended from the living room and kitchen, but that also had its own outside door so she could move about as she wished without feeling as though she was entering someone else's home. The gesture, though unnecessary in her mind, was still thoughtful and appreciated.

Moira had been busy, but not in the way that many brides might have been. Rather than needing linens or hand-stitched items for her new household, she was plotting the location of her garden, as well as a thriving business in cattle grazing. Other settlers on the prairie would pay to graze off her claim, she'd found, especially because there was no danger of a crop being destroyed. She'd already had requests from two homesteaders to board their small herds of livestock on her place while they traveled back east to retrieve their families, with both offering payment in hay and fence work. It was intriguing how the barter system worked among the settlers, and among people who knew the feel of having to pull together for survival.

"Are you sure I don't have to bring in a full harvest?" Moira asked, her brows creasing in concentration as she looked through the claim's paperwork for the hundredth time. "I remember clearly that you said I had to build a fence and provide so much in harvest to be considered a legitimate claim."

"You will have a harvest, only yours will be hay. You can grow hay on your land quite well because it doesn't grow in the saw rows wheat or corn require. Plus, you'll be a livestock breeder, a farmer of animals instead of crops. So long as you can show that you're increasing with each season, it counts. It's only if you tried to pass off the same sad three cows each year that they would wonder if your farm was active."

"I plan to do more than just raise three 'sad' cows! I think I'd actually like to raise horses, much like my fine horse back in Brennan. Those were some of the happiest hours of my week when I got to ride, and days that it wasn't permitted, I would simply pay her a visit in the stables, grooming her and talking with her. She was my dearest companion in times when I thought I had no one, mostly after my mother died."

"How did your mother die, if you don't mind my asking?"

"Oh, not at all. She was always a frail person, having had a childhood illness that robbed her of her strength. But she was the kindest person who ever drew breath, generous to a fault and always concerned with the welfare of anyone within her eyesight. It was she who taught me about the role that we must play to our servants and our common folk, that we are their protectors and their providers."

"Don't they provide for you, you mean? They provide a portion of their crops or face judgment, and they provide their taxes to you, no?"

"Yes, and we're the ones to see to it that their roads are passable, that their business dealings are always fair, and that their voices are heard in government," she reminded him kindly. "I admit, it's a situation I took for granted for many years, and that living here has made me question what I've always just assumed to be a right and fair system."

The only source of discord between Moira and Pryor had been over the house Nathaniel had started. Moira wanted it completed, given that the house was mostly finished and the necessary lumber was sitting around the property, going to waste in the elements. Pryor, who saw no need for his wife to need a home of her own a few miles away, urged her to put the lumber and the effort into completing the rest of her fence before Nathaniel's deadline came due. Moira finally had her way of it with her explanation.

"I've been thinking a good bit about how you felt toward Gretchen when we first came. You were appalled that she would choose to be a servant, and were convinced she served against her will. Although I'm not saying I agree with you, being in Montana has made me question her role now that she's in America and no longer a part of the household at Brennan Castle." Moira paused to make sure that Gretchen wasn't within earshot. "I want to give her the house and a bit of the land outright when she decides to marry."

"Give it to her? But what good would it do her without suitable land to farm it?" Pryor asked.

"The same as it's doing now. It can be grazing land, she could breed and sell livestock; for all we know, she may end up as a teacher, a seamstress, a nurse... perhaps she'll marry a pastor and we'll bring Godliness to the frontier. This is America, after all!" Her eyes twinkled with delight at her fun, but Pryor was impressed with her generosity. He nodded his consent, and agreed to begin work on the house.

Moira had had one other order of business to attend to before she could marry Pryor: she had to let her brother know. She sat down to draft a letter a hundred times, but could not bring herself to explain that she was marrying a man he hadn't chosen for her, and one who had no noble blood. She put aside thoughts of her mother and father and what they must think of her situation, deciding that dwelling on what couldn't be was fruitless. She eventually penned a brief note, informing Ronan that all was well and that she would be marrying at the end of the month.

Now, Pryor helped Moira up into the carriage tenderly before offering a hand to Gretchen, who would serve as a witness to the ceremony in New Hope. Nathaniel had arrived earlier that morning to accompany them and serve as the other necessary witness. Moira shot Gretchen a knowing, hinting look when Nathaniel sat near her in the wagon, but the maid only rolled her eyes.

They chatted happily throughout the long drive to the

town, talking about the spring season ahead of them and their plans for planting. Nathaniel talked as excitedly as always about his plans for his new piece of property, already plotting both his crop and his own modest garden. He'd already begun to set aside his earnings for a breeding pair of horses, and a small stable of cattle. Gretchen, who rarely spoke up in the presence of company, suggested a pig for the return on the meat and the lard for cooking through the year.

"And a pig will eat your scraps, which will help to keep the bears away," she suggested before remembering that she was more comfortable watching others' conversations.

Nathaniel turned to her, impressed with her knowledge. "Did you work a farm then?" he asked, waiting intently for her answer. Gretchen only shook her head, but Moira intervened to save her from answering, explaining what Pryor had had to teach her during their argument shortly after her arrival on his property before changing the subject.

"Mr. Russell, you haven't told us your ideas for hunting this year. What do you think of the stag population? I've always heard they were prized for their antlers, but would you not think the does are the more tender meat?"

Nathaniel turned his attention to a lively discussion of the hunting to be had in the Montana territory, as well as the recent talk that that Indians would refuse to conduct trade with any hunters who took a doe or stag outside of their recommended breeding times. Gretchen looked gratefully at her mistress, silently thanking her for saving her from being the center of attention.

They reached the town in a matter of a couple of hours, and Moira's nerves immediately began to flutter. She'd been in the region for nearly two months, and in America for almost three. She'd crossed not only an ocean but also an entire continent's worth of land, but this was still by far the most frightening thing she'd done. She was about to pledge herself to another person for the rest of their lives, and was doing so without the knowledge or permission of the one person who mattered most to her, outside of Pryor.

"I'll stop in at Jorgenson's and see if there is any news or post," Pryor said, leaning over to speak in her ear. "Do you have need of anything? Anything at all? Just say it, and Jorge can get it for us." Moira shook her head, and Pryor took her hand, holding it in his briefly before kissing the back of it. He released her hand just as quickly and climbed down from the wagon, leaving Gretchen and Moira to watch after the two men as they went to the mercantile.

"Are you sure about this, my lady?" Gretchen finally asked, still watching the two men's backs.

"Now is a fine time to ask me that, dear!" Moira said hollowly, but inside, she was overjoyed. She was only minutes away from marrying Pryor, and it was a decision that she had been more sure of than any she'd made in a long time. This was why she was in Montana, she was sure of it. She had crossed an ocean for him, and it was right.

Soon, though, Pryor returned to the wagon without Nathaniel, having left him in the general store. He held a flat package in his hands and held it out to Moira when he reached the wagon.

"Jorge says this is for you," he said, holding out the thick ivory paper. Moira took it and looked it over, then turned her attention to Gretchen. She dismissed the maid with a slight motion of her head, then waited for the girl to scamper down from the wagon in an obedient gesture that still seemed to amaze Pryor.

"My lady! You must have a bouquet of flowers for your wedding day! I'll arrange it, you'll see!" she cried, looking back once to see that her mistress was all right, then turning and walking away, giving the couple their privacy. After Gretchen was some distance away, Moira patted the wagon seat beside her and gestured for Pryor to join her.

"I have a question to ask you, and it is of no importance other than to sate my own womanly curiosity," she began, looking down at the package without seeing it. Pryor waited expectantly for her to continue. She looked away so as not to direct her question to his still eager face before asking softly, "Can you not read, Pry?"

"No, I can't. Does that matter to you?" he asked, genuine in his answer and unashamed as well.

"Of course not. Not in the least. But... do you wish to be able to read?"

"I hadn't thought of it, to be honest. I don't need to read to know how to plant my crops or birth my livestock, and reading never taught me how to face my cabin away from the wind to keep the cold out. I suppose it would be a helpful thing to know I'm not being taken for a fool in business, but from day to day, I have no need of letters." He stopped and raised Moira's downcast chin with a gentle fingertip. "Does that shame you?"

Moira clasped both of Pryor's hands in hers. "Never! There is naught you could do that could shame me! Not ever!" Her desire to prove her pride in her husband made her grow bolder, and she pressed both of his hands to her warm lips. "If you did wish to know your letters, I would be honored to help you. But if you have no need, then it is naught anyone's say in the matter. And I will be here if you did have need someday. I will read for you."

Pryor smiled with relief, knowing there was no more need to keep any secrets from his wife. "Are you ready to find the county clerk?" Moira nodded. "Then let us find

Nathaniel and this bouquet of yours!"

"Oh, I didn't even open this letter. I'm sure 'tis about the claim," she said, holding Pryor back as she reached for the letter. She turned over the heavy paper and stopped when she saw the familiar wax seal. She tore it open and slid a thick folded sheet from the envelope. She smoothed it out and held it closer, then nearly fainted from the sight of the handwriting she would have recognized anywhere.

It was written in her brother's hand.

CHAPTER TWENTY

Dearest sister,

I pray this letter reaches you, and I pray that it finds you well in body and spirit. You cannot know what has transpired in the time since you left me, and I can only hope that honest men have been truthful with me and will deliver my words to you.

I live in grievous fear that the worst has befallen you. Our uncle, may he eternally rot, contrived for your kidnapping once you left Brennan Castle. He sold you into marriage to a faceless, penniless stranger somewhere in the Americas as punishment for not aligning with that traitor Macomby. His efforts to lay claim to our fortunes have proven for naught, as the king himself has intervened to see that just punishment befalls our father's murderer.

Yes, our father was poisoned by his own brother, a thief intent on gaining all that he could from the family's fortunes. He was not content with the fair dealings our father's future will would stipulate, and sought to destroy our father first in body, then in heritage as he disposed of us. It is only by our good fortune that an accomplice within Uncle's household has come forward and given testimony.

If this letter finds you well, or finds you at all, I beg you to come home. Brennan awaits you, and I await the opportunity to look upon my dear little sister again. There is naught that anyone can do to divide our household now, and I look forward to reuniting again as a family. I pray that you are well and happy, and that my correspondence does not reach you too late.

Loving forever, your brother,

Ronan, Lord Brennan

"My lady?" Gretchen asked softly as she reached the wagon. She laid a thin cluster of delicate purple and white blooms on the wagon seat, all she could find because of the late winter weather, then gently put a hand on her mistress' arm. Moira didn't look at her, instead looking at the paper in her lap and watching as her tears slipped from her cheeks and splashed on the letter, running the ink into small pools. Gretchen peeked at the handwriting and saw Lord Brennan's name and seal. "Oh, dear Lord, spare us! Say 'tis not bad news from home!"

Moira shook her head, but couldn't speak. She passed the letter to Gretchen, who read it eagerly, pressing her hand to her mouth in shock before she'd even read the first third of the page. Pryor looked between them, and gauged that something was wrong even before they had begun speaking rapidly in Irish, the strange brogue-filled words sounding ominous. Instead of interrupting, he let them finish talking; if they weren't using their English, he knew there must be a reason.

Finally, Moira turned to Pryor and began to explain. "The letter is from my brother…"

"The one who was supposed to duel over you? Is he okay?"

"He is," she answered, nodding. "There was a plot between my uncle and a handful of others, a plot to gain the inheritance of Brennan Castle. You were right about my uncle and his involvement with sending me to be your bride. Once I left home, Uncle worked through some contacts in America—that sniveling clerk in the land office, to be sure—to send me out to you instead of to my claim. That plot, and the false betrothal that would have led to the duel you spoke of, have been discovered and thwarted, the saints be praised."

"Oh, well then, this is good news! What a great thing to find out on your wedding day!" Pryor said cheerfully, though his smile faded when he saw that Moira didn't return his excitement, and that fresh tears lid down her pale face. She shook her head. "It isn't good news, my dear? Or… it isn't your wedding day?" He held his breath while he waited for her to answer.

"Pry, I'm… I'm so sorry…"

He held up a hand to stop her from saying anything more. "You don't have to explain. I know what you've been through and I know that coming here was never your choice. You're free to go home now, what person wouldn't choose that? You can have your family and your pretty castle again, so you don't need a cabin in Montana with a husband who doesn't know his letters. Heck, even your servant girl can read, and I can't. No, it's better this way. Go home, Moira, go back to your old life. This one isn't what you want."

He turned and walked away, the soles of his boots scuffing the hard frozen ground. Gretchen turned to admonish Moira.

"What do you think you're doing, miss?" she hissed, keeping her voice low so Pryor wouldn't hear. She looked up and saw that Nathaniel had caught up to him, and the look of happy pride on his face quickly melted into surprise then hurt as Pryor explained what had transpired. "What will you do?"

"It is as my brother has said. He wants me to return to Brennan; he wasn't at all angry in his letter!"

"Angry? Your brother? What right would your brother have to be angry, if you'll pardon my asking, ma'am?"

"Why, he has every right! I ran from my home and left him to fend for himself, not only in the care of our estate, but in all the horrible goings on! He would be within his rights to cast me out and never speak of me again, but instead, he has begged me to come home! That is why I must return at once!"

"And what of Mr. MacAteer?" she asked in a solemn voice.

"What of him?" Moira asked, holding back more tears and even more pain. She knew what he must be feeling at that moment, because she was feeling every bit of the hurt and loss that had been written on his face before he turned away.

"My lady, you can naw let him go! 'Tis a good man, he is, and you clearly care for him. There is respect and affection twixt you, and you would let that go by the wayside to return to Ireland? And to what? What is waiting for you in Brennan 'tis worth losing Mr. MacAteer?"

"Gretchen, that is our home, how can you even ask if there's anything of worth about it?"

"No, my lady, 'tis not me home any longer. 'Twas only me home when I did naw know better, when I did naw know that I could wake up each day and be asked to fetch a breakfast, rather than expected."

"Are you now turning your back on me, too, then? You're leaving me as well, all because I wish to look upon my brother and my home again?"

"Aye miss, that I am," Gretchen answered coldly. "If you would have me choose a life of serving, only to watch you be sold off to another strange husband when the suitable deal happens along, then I'll take my chances on the frontier. Have you considered that? Do you truly not know that you escaped from having to marry a filthy old man, and now you're running back home so your brother can choose for you another husband?"

Moira didn't answer. She looked away, watching Pryor's back. Nathaniel put a hand on his shoulder to comfort him, but Pryor only shook his head. The scene blurred when her eyes flooded with tears again as she watched the broken man in the distance.

Once, her life had been so easy, and not only because she rarely had to lift a finger for her own care. Certainly the servants and her status as a lady had kept her in a life of comfort; she had only to ring a bell or call out a request, and serving boy and nobleman alike bowed to her will. The trade off, though, was the knowledge that her life was not her own to do with as she chose. She had always known that her father, and later, her brother, would be tasked with making a suitable match for her. She had never questioned it, and, in fact, had always welcomed that knowledge.

It was as it should be. As men, they had far more opportunity to meet eligible matches, but even more important, they were privy to the real character of the men they knew. She, however, was only made aware of their courtly manners and their ability to dance at parties. Any conversations she had around men were limited to the weather or poetry or the finer differences between Spanish lace and Belgian lace. It only made sense that they should be the ones to choose, as they knew which men were to be trusted, which ones were a little too fond of drink, and which ones would bring scandal and ruin on her with unscrupulous business dealings.

Now, she couldn't imagine going home and having her hand offered in marriage, not after experiencing the freedom to make her own decisions... and her own mistakes. It was as her maid had said: she'd narrowly escaped marriage to a stranger twice now, so what made her so willing to run back to Ireland, back to the life of a spoiled but captive lady?

"I don't know what to do, Gretchen," she whispered. "I miss my brother so much that it pains my heart, but I cannot leave Pryor. His happiness means the world to me, and for the first time in my life, I know he is one person who genuinely values my happiness as well. Not because he has to," she said, nodding towards her servant. "But because it also brings him joy."

"I can naw tell you what you must do, my lady," her maid said with a comforting smile, her former mirth having burned itself out. "But I can tell you this much: if you go back to Brennan, there will always be a part of you here, a part you've gone and left on the frontier. And you will spend the rest'a your life grieving because you're no longer whole."

"When did you become so wise, Gretchen?" Moira asked, smiling and wiping away her tears with her handkerchief. "If you'll pardon me for being so bold," she teased the younger girl. "I have a husband to claim."

Moira jumped down from the wagon on her own and raced toward Pryor. Nathaniel's eyes went wide at seeing her run toward them, her full skirt flying behind her as her slippered feet danced over the icy ground. He stepped away as Pryor turned toward the sound of her voice, calling out to him.

"Pryor! My dear! I want to marry you! Today, right this very minute, I want us to be married!" She waited with a breathless smile for him to respond, but instead, he narrowed his eyes and regarded her coldly. He didn't speak, he simply watched her eyes as the joy dissolved out of them.

"You've denied me twice, Moira. Why should I believe you want me now?"

CHAPTER TWENTY-ONE

Moira's face fell as Pryor's meaning settled on her. Instead of sharing her elation, he had already hardened his heart against her, as surely as the winter ground was hard. She had no one to blame but herself, she knew it, for his words were true. She'd refused his generosity in bringing her to New Hope, and she'd refused him now when she chose her brother and her estate over a life lived with him on his simple but prosperous farm.

"Pry, I do care about you. I... I love you. I had hoped you felt the same way."

"I do. Or maybe I did. But you are not a woman of your word. When you first broke our engagement, I could understand. There was the whole trickery with your uncle, and you proved that you were not the one to enter the contract. I forgave the whole thing and even welcomed you into my home.

"But then, today, you went back on your word again, all because of a letter? I don't even know what it truly says, but

132

whatever it is, it was worth going back on your word to me. Those words were more important than our agreement. How am I to know that there won't be something else to make you break your word again?"

"Pryor, I will not. Surely you understand my confusion and my hurt, but it was only momentary! I saw reason, and have seen that you are the choice I want to make. I don't want to be in Ireland, I want to be here... with you."

"Are you only saying that because you have no way home, or do you really mean it?"

"I mean it with my whole heart, Pry. And I thank you to remember that I do have a way back; I could buy my passage right this very moment. For that matter, I could sell my claim and live anywhere I choose." She took a step toward him and reached for his hand, holding it tightly in both of hers. He didn't respond as his rough fingers lay unmoving in her small hands, but he didn't pull his hand away, either, an encouraging sign. "Pry, I choose to be with you."

His expression softened ever so slightly, even if his eyes did not brighten with any sign of warmth. He pondered her statement for a long time, but Moira was resolute. She would wait for as long as it took, willing him to say something. Whether it was news her heart wanted to hear or not, she would wait.

He looked about to speak when the rumbling sound of the train came from the east. Was it already the proscribed time, the day Pryor had told her he would return her to the train so she could move on? What a strange turn of events that would find her standing so close to the depot on just this very day. The ominous coincidence was heartbreaking; would Pryor take this as a sign that she should leave?

I'm not going anywhere! Moira thought fiercely. *Whether*

Pryor returns my love or not, I will stay in Montana, I will develop my claim, and I will live the rest of my life as a woman of the frontier, free to live as I choose!

"Moira, I do love you," he answered over the sound of metal wheels grating against the steel tracks, the brakes working as hard as they might to slow the massive beast.

"But you do not wish me to stay?" she asked slowly, heading off his answer.

"I do! But I cannot listen to any more promises if you're not going to see them through. My sensibilities and my heart can't take it. If you're to stay—with me, I mean, so think of it carefully—you have to mean that you're staying for good. I don't know what I'll do if you leave me."

Moira closed her eyes with relief, smiling as she nodded. She looked to answer him, to tell him that he would never have to worry that she would leave, but a movement behind him caught her attention. She stared intently at the figure as it moved closer, then pushed past Pryor to walk toward the approaching man. Before she'd taken three steps, she broke into a run, her wool bonnet flying off in her haste to reach him. When she stood before him, she looked intently at his face before throwing herself in his arms.

"Ronan! But... but I do not understand! How? How is it possible that you're here?" she stammered, the tension in her bones melting away when he put his arms around her, too.

"I've been looking for you, dear sister! When I heard what happened, where you'd gone... I was ready to take up our father's pistols and call out Macomby all the same! And that wretched uncle of ours! Oh, Moira, I cannot believe I found you! The man at the land office—this Mr. Walsh, who dealt with you so grievously—gave me the necessary information to try to locate you. I finally decided the only way to find you was to look for you myself, so I began with the train that should have taken you West." He held her closer and bent down to kiss her on the forehead. "Oh, it's taken me two months of looking, and here you are! I cannot believe I've found you, and you're safe! Are you well? Have you been ill? Injured? Treated poorly?"

Moira shook her head. "No, Ronan, all is well! I've had such an adventure, but I'm safe and happy. And you've arrived in time for my wedding day! It was in my letter!" She turned and indicated Pryor, who stood awkwardly in the distance watching the pair, unable to hear their words.

Ronan looked at his sister sharply and reverted to Irish, shaking his head. "I never received a letter. But married? What is this? I've come to return you to Brennan, to save you from this plot our uncle cooked up. I won't see you left behind and forced into marriage."

"No, brother, that is not the way of it. I came here of my own accord, I signed on to homestead a claim! I am a land owner now, quite the land baroness, if I say so! But marrying was my choice, not anything inflicted on me."

Ronan looked confused, then turned his gaze to Pryor. "Is this the man Uncle mandated? I'll kill him myself for his part in stealing you from us."

"No! Ronan, look at me. I promise, it is as I say..."

"You do not have to stay just because you've... been ruined... by their evil ways," he answered, looking around furtively and whispering his words directly in her ear so that no one could hear them. "I promise you, we will never speak of it, and it will be as if it never happened."

"Brother!" Moira cried, her cheeks turning a deep shade of crimson. "No! It is not that way! I swear it! How could you ask—"

"My dear sister, I am sorry, I did not mean to make you cry! I only meant to reassure you, but if it is as you say, I do believe you. I promise you." Ronan hugged Moira tightly again, whispering his apologies over and over. At the sight of her upset, Pryor came forward, prepared to call out this strange man if need be.

"Moira? Dear? Are you all right?" he asked gruffly, prepared to hate the man who'd made his bride cry. Moira turned and forced a smile for Pryor's sake before remembering that this was truly a happy occasion. Her brother stood miraculously before her, and her groom waited to make her his wife. There was no more joyous occasion anywhere in Montana than at that very moment in New Hope.

"Pry, of course! This is my brother, Ronan, Lord Brennan. Brother, this is Pryor MacAteer, soon to be my husband, if you'll give us your blessing." Both men turned to Moira in astonishment, Ronan because this was such an unorthodox marriage process for a lady of Moira's station, and Pryor because he was intent on marrying his bride that day, blessing from her brother or no. She smiled broadly at both of them and waited as they begrudgingly shook hands and stated their greetings.

"Ronan... my brother... say you'll come with us to the wedding. We're to go to the cabin and have a feast afterward, please come!" She shot him a roguish grin. "Besides, there's nowhere else to stay, as I learned the moment I stepped down from the train!"

Ronan looked back and forth between Pryor and Moira, taking in their plain attire but their happy, eager expressions. This was not the way he'd envisioned his younger sister leaving his household to wed, but even had to admit that this was a far more jubilant bride than any other he'd seen.

"Mr. MacAteer," Ronan began grimly. "Are you marrying my sister because she's a woman of means? Or do you have genuine affection for each other?" Pryor paused, unwilling to dignify the accusation with an answer. He leveled his gaze at Ronan and waited for him to ask what he wanted to know in a way that wasn't so insulting. His lordship, on the other hand, was more accustomed to staring men down than Pryor, and he waited in kind.

"I am marrying her because I care for her," Pryor finally replied with a note of finality that plainly said he was not going to entertain any more questions of the sort. "She is kind, and smart, and funny, and her being here makes me happy. If she was a woman of means before we met, then I have to venture a guess that she still will be. But it won't have anything to do with me."

Ronan curtly nodded his approval of Pryor's answer then looked his sister. "Moira, are you marrying this man just so you don't have to come home and be the lady of Brennan Castle? Because if that's your reason, I assure you, I will not let you fall into some elderly brute's clutches. You will have a say in whom you marry, if you marry at all."

Moira looked to Pryor, realizing that this was Ronan's test for them before he bestowed his blessing on their match. She sighed, and answered, "I am marrying Pryor because I adore him. He is generous and concerned with the welfare of others, to a fault, I must say. He lives a simple existence out on this frontier, but he does so because it brings him happiness, not because he cannot fare better elsewhere. I've been a noble lady my whole life, and it hasn't fared me too well so far... it's time I lived a more common life, one that looks for the joy of simplicity instead of excess."

Ronan nodded again at her answer, then hesitantly pronounced his permission on their marriage. Moira beamed, although Pryor looked somewhat put out that this stranger—who had found them by sheer, stupid coincidence—deigned to oversee their wedding and declare it fit and proper.

"Now then," Ronan called out in a booming voice befitting the lord of a castle. "Let's get you to the church and secure this marriage!"

CHAPTER TWENTY-TWO

Among the many other things that New Hope didn't have—a sheriff, a boarding house, a restaurant or kitchen to take one's meals—the town didn't have a church or a pastor. A circuit riding pastor came once every other month, long enough to teach the masses to give to the government what was the government's, and to take up an offering collection, of course.

So that is the reason Pryor and Moira found themselves standing on the porch of the government clerk's office, exchanging promises to be faithful and caring. Nathaniel, in his ever-present excitement about nearly everything, had told a good number of settlers about the wedding, so it was very nearly a county fair-sized celebration that turned out for their ceremony. The proceedings consisted of a few brief words spoken in prayer over the couple and over the pending harvest for all farmers present, then their signing the license with their marks that they were who they said that they were, and that they were now married.

The couple stepped down from the front porch of the clerk's low building. They shook hands with all of the well-wishers from the surrounding claims who'd come out specifically to celebrate. The farmers could read a sky as well as any seafarer, so they didn't linger long in town because of the eerie clouds that hung over the town, threatening to dump snow on them again despite the fact that the last batch still hadn't melted off all of the buildings and rooftops.

Pryor, Moira, and their smaller group of guests stepped across the wide cattle path and entered Jorgenson's store, the men ducking nearly to their shoulders to get inside. They exchanged pleasantries and received hearty congratulations from the shopkeeper, who was already demanding to know when to expect young ones. He sent them off with a wedding gift of a basket of fresh fruit, brought in on the very train that had carried Ronan to them.

The wagonload of passengers chatted happily all the way back to Pryor's cabin. When they arrived, Ronan immediately took in the view of the MacAteer farm, and had to admit he was impressed. The home, though nothing like the grand castle that had existed in the Brennan family for more than three hundred years, was well-suited to raising both a family and a valley full of crops and livestock.

"My sister, it is my hope that you will be happy here," he said in a moment of stolen words. Moira returned his smile, and nodded.

"And it is my hope that you will come back here someday, any day. I have long had plans for land in America." She began to explain to him her ideas for establishing the Brennan family in this new part of the country, and watched as his look moved from mere amusement at his little sister's business acumen, to genuine respect for her talents and head for industry.

The group ate and talked and laughed for the better part of the day, breaking only long enough for the men to see to the chores and the animals and the ladies to cook a filling meal. By dinnertime, Gretchen and Moira had prepared a small feast, compromised of dainty cakes and breads, vegetables from the cellar, a hearty soup of potatoes whose recipe had come all the way from Ireland with them, and a succulent pig that Pryor had butchered and roasted over a pit in the yard for the occasion. It was nothing like the parties Moira had once planned and proudly presented in Ireland, lacking the refinement of well-bred ladies and gentlemen, and lacking the genteel dancing to music provided by visiting court composers from all over Europe, but she would not have traded this simple festivity for any of those lavish affairs.

By evening, the group was ready to disperse for the night. Nathaniel set out for his small, newly-finished home, and politely invited Ronan to stay with him and inspect his claim, casting a quick, surreptitious glance in Gretchen's direction. Ronan quickly understood and took him up on his offer. For her part, Gretchen insisted there was important work still to be done on the new cabin on Moira's claim, work that had to begin early the next morning if she hoped to ever finish it all, and she made ready to set off on one of Pryor's horses for the short trip. Moira helped her wrap in blankets and scarves, but before the maid left, she grabbed her mistress in a tight embrace, weeping silent tears of elation for Moira.

"My lady, I am so proud for you. My heart is near to bursting for your happiness. I know this is naw the match you thought for yourself, nor that your dear mother would have thought for you, but it is a good match, all the same. I know you will be much blessed in your marriage, and find much to love about Mr. MacAteer... and Montana."

"Why, Gretchen! You sound like you're leaving on a journey instead of popping over to the neighboring farm!" Moira cried, a feeling of alarm traveling through her and cooling her delight slightly. "I fully expect to see you tomorrow, dear!"

"And 'twill be so, for now. But you are a married woman now, and a landowner. You do naw have need of a serving girl to braid your hair or do up your stays or lace your gown before the party!" Gretchen smiled weakly. "I had thought to return to Ireland with Lord Brennan and resume my duties in the household, but I could never abandon you here, never knowing what befalls you, never having a familiar face to meet with just to exchange a kind word or two. No, I promise you, I will be here so long as you have need of me, but I fear you'll find I'm needed no longer."

Moira grabbed Gretchen and held her close, not speaking for several minutes. When she stepped back, new tears, both from the bliss of the day and from fear of losing the person she'd been closest to her entire life, ran afresh.

"Then I now pronounce you my servant no longer... now you are but my friend, my dearest, most wonderful friend! And I cannot lose you! Come see me tomorrow and we will describe new terms for you. You know, if I am to live here on Pryor's claim, then I will need an overseer—on salary, of course, and with lodgings—to run my vast estate here in Montana!" They both laughed at the description of Moira's simple homestead as her estate, but Gretchen nodded, promising Moira she would return late the very next day.

Moira waved from the wide porch of the cabin, watching her friend until she was out of sight. She almost didn't hear Pryor walk up behind her, but she warmed instantly at the touch of his hands on her shoulders, thrilled at the slight pressure of their weight even through the thick wrap she wore to stave off the cold. She reached both her hands up and held one of his, letting herself lean back against the solid wall of his chest. When she turned her face up to look at his, she saw an expression of pure contentment there.

Moira turned to face her husband and gave him a wry glance. "Do you take me at my word now?"

"What word is that, wife?" he asked skeptically, but did so with a merry look in his bright eyes.

"My word that I will be your wife, that I will live here and be a source of help and comfort, and that I will love you for the rest of our days." Pryor threw back his head and laughed, a sound Moira swore she could hear echoing throughout their valley. He pulled her close to him, pressing her against his chest as he wound his arms around her.

"Whatever am I going to do with a wife so fine as you? There are no servants here to do our bidding, remember? Not unless you count the goats in the barn, and I'm afraid they're just too stupid to be of any use around the house."

"I don't want my servants, or my gowns, or my castle. This is what I want. A place of my own, with a husband that I chose by my side. You didn't wish to marry me because I could secure your family's lands or provide an heir for your title or because I came with a handsome dowry, and that's all that matters to me."

Pryor looked at Moira hesitantly, then leaned close to her. She knew what he was after and turned her chin up to his, meeting him as he closed the scant distance between them. He pressed his lips to hers softly, the nervousness they both felt taking its time in melting away as they discovered each other.

"I've wanted to do that since the day you stepped off the train," he finally whispered, taking both her hands in his and pulling her into the house. Moira blushed slightly, but smiled.

"And I'm so glad the moment has finally come that you can," she answered truthfully.

"So, Lady Moira," he teased, shutting the door behind them and latching it tight before enfolding her in his strong arms again. "You say you're ready for this new life as a farmer and homesteader?"

"That I am, but there shall be no more titles for me...other than missus, of course! Mrs. MacAteer, the happiest wife in Montana!"

THE END

Thank you for reading and supporting my book and I hope you enjoyed it.

Please will you do me a favor and leave me a review. It would be very much appreciated, thank you.

OTHER BOOKS BY AMELIA ROSE

Learning To Love (Carson Hill Ranch: Book 1)
Carson Hill Ranch (Trilogy Bundle Box Set)
Silver River Romeo (Rancher Romance: Book 1)
Stranded, Stalked and Finally Sated)
(License To Love: Book 1)
Silver Heart (Longren Family: Book 1)
Mending Fences (Texas Heat: Book 1)

CONNECT WITH AMELIA ROSE

Feel free to visit my website at **www.ameliarose.info** to sign up to my newsletter so that you will be notified as to when my new releases are available.

ABOUT
AMELIA ROSE

Amelia is a shameless romance addict with no intentions of ever kicking the habit. Growing up she dreamed of entertaining people and taking them on fantastical journeys with her acting abilities, until she came to the realization as a college sophomore that she had none to speak of. Another ten years would pass before she discovered a different means to accomplishing the same dream: writing stories of love and passion for addicts just like herself. Amelia has always loved romance stories and she tries to tie all the elements she likes about them into her writing.

Made in the USA
Monee, IL
13 November 2021

82063509R00090